The Air Mystery of Isle La Motte

Edith Janice Craine

This is the first book of the Sky Buddies, Jim Austin and Bob Caldwell and their plane, properly christened "HER HIGHNESS" in which they encounter many thrilling and exciting adventures.

Originally published 1930

TABLE OF CONTENTS

XII
DETECTIVES

I
THE STEP-BROTHERS

"I say now, why are you fellows landing here?" The Canadian Mounted Policeman reined in his horse as close to the cock-pit as he could get, and eyed the two occupants in the plane, which had just landed in the southern part of the Province of Quebec.

"You want the truth, the whole truth, and nothing but the truth?" the blue-eyed youth in the passenger's seat drawled in an accent that could belong to only one part of the world, Texas.

"If you're telling it today," the mounty replied. "If not, we'll get it later."

"Very true, but you shall have it pronto. From an elevation of three thousand feet we observed you, so we came down to find out if you are riding a real horse, or merely an imitation—"

"It isn't a bad plug," interrupted the pilot, whose eyes were blue and they rested with approval on the animal that had aroused their curiosity. "But, if you ever visit Cap Bock, we'll fork you on something superior—we have a pinto that can—"

"Now, look here, I'm not fooling. You hop out of that and give an account of yourselves," the mounty ordered firmly.

"Yes, sir." The two obeyed willingly enough and the man dismounted. When they took off their helmets he saw they were boys, both had tow heads, and they didn't look at all formidable or like a pair he might have to escort to headquarters. However, duty was duty and he wasn't making any snap judgments or taking needless risks. There was too much smuggling, to say nothing of illegal immigration across the border, and orders were strict. It was not at all outside possibility that a couple of perfectly innocent looking youths might be the tools or employees of some powerful gang. The fact that they dropped out of the skies in an airplane was in itself suspicious.

"I'm Jim Austin, age sixteen years and two months. This is my step-brother, Bob Caldwell, fifteen years and eleven months," the grey-eyed boy announced gravely.

"Proud to meet you, sir," Bob bowed, then added. "I'm almost as old as he is."

"Well, go ahead, get along with the story," the mounty put in more pleasantly. His horse had walked close to the boy and was nosing about the pockets of his aviation coat. Soberly Bob drew forth an apple, broke it in half and fed the big fellow.

"We were both born with a complete pair of parents on ranches, adjoining ones, along Cap Rock in Texas, but circumstances, over which we had no control removed my mother and Bob's father," Jim explained. "When I was twelve I discovered that my father was spending a lot of time on the Caldwell ranch and I lay awake nights wondering why a Texas gentleman couldn't shoot a lady."

"And I planned to set a trap for Mr. Austin and fill him full of lead," Bob offered. "Give me your apple, Jim." Jim handed it over without hesitation and it was fed to the horse.

"Then, one day, I happened along by the water-hole and found some Greasers knocking the stuffing out of Bob. We beat them off, and after that, I went to the Caldwell's. It was a nice, clean house and Mrs. Caldwell gave me a square meal; woman cooked."

"My mother is the best cook in Texas," Bob offered softly.

"Yes. That night I started to follow my father and I ran into Bob. We rode about and talked it over. Bob's mother wanted him to go to school."

"And Bob didn't want to," the officer suggested solemnly.

"Oh yes I did," Bob replied quickly.

"But a mother, ranch, a string of horses and a pair of blue cranes, is a responsibility," Jim offered, "Then, we rode to the house—"

"And found his father eating a piece of chocolate cake that I didn't know anything about," said Bob.

"And he'd eaten the last crumbs," Jim added. "Then, we told them they were a pair of boobs. A week later the knots were tied that united the ranches and made us step-brothers. We were all at our place—"

"And Bob was to be sent to school?"

"Sure, but his mother said I had to go too," Jim grinned.

"Not so good."

"It was not so bad because his father said that when we finished the course, it was four years, we could have an airplane, he'd see that we were properly instructed in its chauffeuring. We were both hipped about flying," Bob answered.

"So we went to the school, did the work in two years and a half, learned piloting on the side, then went home and made the old man keep his word. Meet Her Highness," he waved his hand toward the plane which was a beauty.

"I'm glad to," the officer grinned broadly. "Now, tell me what you are doing here."

"You haven't told us anything about yourself," Bob reminded him.

"Later."

"Bob's mother has a sister, Mrs. Norman Fenton, and she lives on a farm on North Hero Island. In the summer time she takes tourists and calls the house, Stumble Inn. We came to see a bit of the world and to pay her a visit. Arrived yesterday and this morning took a hop over British soil. We like it even if it isn't Texas."

"That's generous of you. I'm Sergeant Bradshaw on border patrol duty, the horse is Patrick. He was imported from one of the western states, don't know which one, but he was a bloody beast when he was wished on me—"

"Somebody had mistreated him," Bob announced. "He's got a scar on his leg. Looks like a short-hitch hobble that cut him." The boy stooped over, took the hoof in his hand and Pat submitted amiably to the inspection.

"Reckon it was done with raw-hide," Jim declared. His fingers gently manipulated the old wound and Pat turned his nose about to sniff at the youngster.

"Pat doesn't usually make friends with strangers. You must have a way with horses," Sergeant Bradshaw told them.

"We came out of the sky to meet him," Bob reminded the man.

"Dad told us before we started north to make our trip as profitable as possible by learning all we can. It's against our principles to ask impudent questions, but we should like to know what you have to do," Jim announced and Bradshaw laughed heartily.

"I have to patrol this territory, watch the roads carefully, and every place where smugglers of any kind might try to break across the border. There has been no end of bootlegging—"

"Thought Canada was all wet," Bob grinned.

"The provinces have local option and Quebec went dry, so we have to enforce it, but the rum runners are the least of our troubles, although they are bad enough. There's a lot of objectionable people sneaking in to both this country and yours, besides drugs and jewelry. This is a pretty wild section and it keeps Pat and me on our toes."

"Noticed from the air it isn't much settled. Didn't know there is so much open space outside of Texas," Bob said.

"I should think you'd have a plane and you could see what's going on a lot better. With the glasses we knew all about what you looked like before we came down," Jim remarked.

"There are some planes on the job, but men and horses are necessary—mighty necessary," the sergeant answered. "The airmen can tell us if anything is moving that is suspicious, but we have to be down here to get it, unless the outlaws are taking the air."

"Anything special afoot now," Jim inquired.

"You bet there is." Both boys looked at him eagerly. "Our men and yours have been working for months trying to get something on a gang that has put it over every time. If we don't make a killing soon, I can see where there will be a general shaking up in both forces and a lot of us will be sent to hoe hay." The officer spoke seriously and the boys listened with keen interest.

"Tell you what, we didn't think we'd find anything very exciting so far north, but I reckon we'll ooze around here and see what we can pick up. Maybe we can help you. You'll recognize Her Highness if you see her sailing through again, and if we want to communicate with you, we'll circle around and drop you a message if we can't land. How will you let us know if you receive it O.K.?"

"That's fine of you, Jim, but this is a man-sized job. I appreciate your offer no end, old top, but your Aunt and Uncle, to say nothing of your mother and father would come down on me hard if I agreed to let you risk your necks—"

"The parents are sensible people, we picked them out for that very reason. They both told us to have a good time, and helping you looks to me like a good time—"

"Besides, what would we risk? All we could do is report to you if we see anything, and like as not what we see won't be much help because we're so green. But, if we did see anything real—because we are such a pair of nuts we might put something over for you. We elect ourselves, you're in the minority, so, if you hear Her Highness, listen, stop, watch. Come on, Buddy, your aunt was making cherry pies when we left and if we don't get a move on, some cadaverous tourist is likely to come along and eat every snitch of it. They are a greedy lot."

"Isn't your aunt the woman who raises such a flock of turkeys?" the sergeant asked.

"Sure, she used to. She has them on Isle La Motte, but last year they didn't do so well, and she said last night that she isn't having much luck this spring. It's tough because there is money in turkeys if you can ever make them grow up," Bob replied.

"I drove down there once and got a couple for my family. They were grand birds. Come on, Pat."

"You haven't told us yet how we will know that you get our message," Jim reminded him.

"I'll wave my hat, and if I want you to come down, I'll keep it off my head, but you fellows watch your step and don't go doing anything that will get us all into the cooler," he warned.

"We'll look out." They both rubbed Pat's nose, then climbed into the cock-pit of Her Highness, this time Bob took the pilot's seat.

"Need any help?"

"Not a bit, thanks." Bob opened her up, the engine bellowed, the propeller spun and Her Highness raced forward, lifted her nose as if sniffing the air, then climbed into it. Jim waved at the man, who wondered if he had not better telephone the Fentons and tell them to keep the boys out of any trouble. On second thought, he decided against it. After all, their own air men were watching from above, and as they were every one of them experts at the game, they would report things long before the boys could possibly have their suspicions aroused. It would be too bad to spoil their fun, and if they would enjoy keeping an eye on the world, let them do it. They appeared to be a pretty decent pair of kids.

"You almost flew off with them, Old Top," he remarked, giving the horse an affectionate pat, "and only yesterday you bared your teeth and scared the wits, what little he has, out of that Canuck. You are a discriminating old cuss." He leaped into the saddle, but he waited to make a note of the meeting of the boys and their account of themselves. "Even at that they may be stringing me," he remarked a bit uneasily as he glanced toward the fast disappearing speck in the sky, but he dismissed the thought immediately for he felt confident the step-brothers were entirely trustworthy.

In the meantime Her Highness climbed in swift spirals for three thousand feet, then Bob leveled her off, set his course and started toward North Hero, which is one of many delightful bits of land in Lake Champlain. Presently the boys could see a tiny shack with the British Flag floating on one side, the Stars and Stripes on the other.

"They look like good pals," Jim said into the speaking tube, and Bob glanced over the side.

"Great pair," he responded. "Not like the border at Texas." He took a good look at the huge lake that stretched out restlessly between New York State and Vermont. "We could use that down our way."

"Let's send some of it to Dad. Remember how long it is?"

"One hundred and twenty-eight miles."

"Bigger than the two ranches together." They flew on until they were flying over the water, and Jim took the glasses to get a better view of the historic lake. He picked out Rouse's Point, then on to the picturesque sections of land whose rocky coasts had defied the pounding waves. There was Isle La Motte, with it's farms at one end and long wooded stretch at the other where the Fenton's kept their turkeys. Beyond, united by a long bridge was North Hero Island, cut up into small homesteads. There were acres of uncultivated land which was now blue and yellow with flowers, groves of cedar, elm and ash, to say nothing of delicate green spots that the boys knew were gardens or meadows. Further on was Grand Isle, also connected by a bridge, but they were not going that far.

"Let's hop down on the turkey end of La Motte," Jim suggested, and Bob nodded. He shut the engine off, let Her Highness glide, and circled for a landing place. "Get on the water." Young Caldwell kicked forward a lever which shifted landing wheels to water floats, selected a smooth cove, and in a moment they lighted, splashed and stopped.

"Hey you, get the heck out of here. Get out!" The voice came from back of a fallen tree, and in a moment a huge man whose face was ugly with anger, walked along the dead bole and shook his fist at them. "Get out. You ain't no business around here."

"We just dropped in to have a look at the turkeys," Bob told him. "We're—" But Jim stepped on his foot.

"What's the matter?" He broke in quickly. "We're not going to hurt anything. We've never seen a turkey farm and we heard that you have a fine one here."

"You're right you're not going to hurt anything, and you're not going to see this turkey farm. Hear! Now, get out! You're on private property and I'll have the law on you! Don't you see them signs, 'No Trespassing', right there!" He pointed to a large sign hung between two trees and it plainly warned off inquisitive, or interested spectators. "Go on, now, get out."

Bob glanced questioningly at his step-brother. He had started to tell the caretaker who they were, feeling sure that the information would naturally assure them a very different reception, but for some reason or other, the older boy wanted to withhold the fact. Just then the man broke off a dry branch, raised it over his head, and prepared to throw it.

"Move out of his range," Jim said tensely. "He might land that in our propeller or tail." Bob sent Her Highness scurrying over the water and the stick fell harmlessly behind the plane.

"The ornery old cuss," Bob growled at the indignity. He whirled the plane about, held her nose low, and set the propeller racing. Instantly it kicked up a spray of water that shot out on all sides, and before the man could move, he was drenched to the skin.

"Confound your hides," he bellowed, but Her Highness was circling away, then she lifted, climbed swiftly and started homeward. Bob taxied her low across the two miles of water, and brought her down close to the boat pier, where she "rode at anchor."

"Boys, dinner's ready." Mrs. Fenton, a typical, tall, slender Vermont woman, came out onto the back veranda of the old house.

"So are we," Bob shouted. The plane made secure, they raced around the curve, across the wide, sloping lawn, up the high stairs, and into the living-room.

"There's basins outside to wash up," Mrs. Fenton told them, and soon they were splashing the cold water over their faces, and lathering their hands with the cake of home-made soap.

"Well, you lads get a good look at Vermont?" Mr. Fenton joined them at his own basin. He too was tall and slender, with kindly grey eyes, and a broad smile. Although they had never seen him before until their arrival twenty-four hours earlier, they both liked him enormously.

"Corking. She's some state, Uncle Norman!" Bob answered from behind the roller towel.

"She's got a lot of her under water," Jim added.

"Expect you'd like some of that in Texas."

"Surely could use it. Cracky, some of those hot spots would seep it up like a sponge."

"We could spare a good deal of it," Mr. Fenton told them. "Especially when it's high."

"Does it get much higher than it is now?" Jim asked.

"It has swelled up fifteen feet more, then it does some flooding, but that doesn't happen often, not so far north, but we get plenty. Well, come on in. Hope you didn't leave your appetites in the sky."

"We did not."

"I will take the milk now, sir." The boys turned quickly at the voice, which was deep and musical, and saw a tall, powerfully built man, whose skin and eyes were dark. He wore the usual overalls, a tan shirt open at the throat, and carried himself more like a person of importance than a working man or a farmer.

"All right, Corso. Here it is waiting for you." Mr. Fenton handed down a covered pail.

"I thank you, sir," Corso replied with dignity.

"Your nephew is doing an interesting job on that mud hole. The boy is a good worker."

"He is learning. We thank you." The man accepted the pail of milk and walked away swiftly. The boys noted that he was amazingly light on his feet for a man of his size.

"Is he a Vermonter, Uncle Norman?" Bob asked as they made they way to the dining room where the table would have groaned if it had not been accustomed to such a bounteous load.

"No, he isn't. I really don't know where he comes from, Bob, and my guess is Spain, although I'm probably miles off on that. He and his young nephew, a boy about thirteen, or perhaps a little older, rented a shack a mile or so up the shore; they paid several months in advance.

Seem to spend their time walking, or on the lake, and I believe I'm about the only person, on North Hero Island Corso talks with, and he doesn't say very much to me. I've seen the boy, of course, but I don't know if he can speak English or not, I've never heard him."

"He's a nice looking boy," Mrs. Fenton put in.

"Ever since they came your aunt has longed to get her motherly hands on him," Mr. Fenton laughed.

"He needs a woman to look after him, see that he gets proper food and plenty of it. He's as thin as a stick, and I know he was sick this spring. I did make Corso take some puddings and jellies to him," she announced.

"They sound like an interesting pair," Jim remarked.

"Well, they are, but they mind their own business, and we Vermonters mind ours. How about it, light meat or dark, Jim?"

"Dark, please."

"What is the boy doing with the mud hole?" Bob wanted to know, for a mud hole didn't sound very promising.

"I don't know what it will be like when he gets finished but I'm keen to see. It's a strip about two and a half acres wide, and five long, that has always been a dead loss for cultivation. It comes between my alfalfa meadow and the garden; dips down low and toward the middle is quite a hole. The place catches all the rain and hangs on to it all through the hottest months. I had an expert here to drain it several years ago, he sunk some pipes, and although he did get the water off, more came back inside of a few weeks, and it was full after the first rain storm. The land is very fertile, and if I could use it, I would raise bumper crops."

"Shame you can't."

"Yes, it is. Corso came to me early this spring, some weeks ago, and asked if I would rent it to him, and permit him to dig and do anything he wanted to with it. He assured me he would do it no harm, nor the surrounding patches. I told him it wasn't good for anything, but he seemed to want it, so I let him have it. He and the boy spend a great deal of time there, and they have hauled a lot of rocks from the shore. You probably noticed the edge of the lake, except around the cliffs, is all small flat stones, not very brittle, but not so soft as soap-stone."

"Sure, we were looking at them last night. Some have pink and white streaks, like marble, and are pretty. I'd like to send a box to Mom for the garden walks. She'd be pleased to pieces to have them."

"They have taken several loads of them and some very large stones. After dinner you might walk over and see what you make out of the work so far. I can't make head or tail of it. A few days ago they planted corn, right in the mud, and in each hole they put a minnow they scooped out of the lake."

"Why put fish in, do they expect to raise sardines?" Jim laughed.

"Can't say," Mr. Fenton answered.

"It's some heathen notion I know." Mrs. Fenton announced positively. "Are you getting enough to eat, Bob?"

II
THE THREE MYSTERIES

"I say, Uncle Norman, you surely have a crab of a man to look after your turkeys," Bob remarked when the noonday meal was nearly finished, and the boy suddenly recalled their very unwelcome reception on Isle La Motte.

"A crab?"

"I'll tell the herd he is the prize long horn for meanness," Jim added emphatically.

"My goodness, boys, what on earth did he do?" Mrs. Fenton asked soberly, as if she could hardly believe her ears.

"He wouldn't let us near the place," Bob explained, then went on with an account of their effort to see the turkey farm.

"Hezzy's all right, boys. You didn't tell him who you were."

"No, we didn't, but great snakes, about everybody on the three islands seemed to know we were coming. Didn't seem reasonable that this fellow did not have an idea who we were," Jim declared.

"Of course, airplane visitors are not common and the news of your arriving from Texas did spread, but it's possible Hezzy didn't hear of it," Mrs. Fenton told them.

"You see, boys, he's been having quite a peck of trouble. Last year they hatched a big flock of birds, but before they were half grown, a lot of them were stolen. We know they didn't die—only a few of them—and there is no way for them to have wandered off. Their wings are clipped as soon as they are big enough to get any height, and turkeys do not fly very high or far, anyway. Some one, or some band of thieves must have made away with them. Hezzy is hired to raise them, I haven't time to and look after the farm, and he takes real pride in having a big flock. Some of the young ones have disappeared already and I expect he's keeping a mighty close watch to save as many as he can. They bring a good price and last year was the first season we didn't realize a profit on them."

"Any idea where they go?"

"No, we haven't, but it must be outsiders. Probably some tourists discovered the old farm tucked away there in the woods, and let it be known, or came back themselves. We have three watchmen, and now one of them sits up all night, but it hasn't done much good," Mr. Fenton answered.

"Sure Hezzy isn't putting his own brand on them?" Jim suggested.

"My goodness sakes alive, child, don't say anything like that. I wouldn't have anyone hear you for the world," Aunt Belle said anxiously.

"Hezzy is too honest for his own good, really. He wouldn't take a bent pin that didn't belong to him. I've known him since I was a boy. He's a fine poultry man and absolutely reliable. Keeps his records as accurate as can be. There isn't a cent's worth he doesn't give a detailed account of every week," Mr. Fenton supplemented.

"I didn't mean to cast reflections on his honesty, but he was such a bear, it just occurred to me he might be feathering his own nest with your turkeys," Jim said.

"Oh, dear me, don't say it again. Why, I should be so distressed to have it get out—"

"We won't breath it, Aunt Belle," Bob promised.

"I'll take you over sometime and you can see the place. I ordered a pair of good watchdogs to help guard it. They should be here in a day or so," Mr. Fenton said, then added. "Well, if you want to go out and inspect what's being done on the mud hole, come along."

"Perhaps they could eat another piece of pie, Norman."

"No, we couldn't, not a sliver," Bob insisted.

"Much to our regret," Jim grinned.

"Very well," Aunt Belle agreed.

The two boys followed Mr. Fenton out of the front door, down the flower lined path under a grove of huge maples, across the road onto the farm proper, past the barns, around the vegetable garden and then he stopped and made a gesture.

"Here it is." They saw the land, much as he had described it, the alfalfa meadow rising gently on the further side, and between them was a long pond of still water which was very dirty.

"Some hole," Jim nodded. They walked on, picking their way until they saw a boy at work, and they stood quietly watching him. He did not realize they were there and went on with his task quite as if he was alone on the island.

"What the heck is he doing?" Bob whispered. The boy had some odd sort of implement, the handles of which he grasped in both hands, stood it upright, then jumped, his feet landing in the middle; driving the queer tool deep into the ground. Then he stepped off, bent the handles as far as they would go, and raised the earth.

"I think it is some sort of shovel, or plow," Mr. Fenton told them, "but I never saw anything like it. Listen and you'll hear him sing, it's a kind of a chant." The step-brothers listened and in a moment they could hear, but the words and melody were unfamiliar. As the youngster straightened up, they could see that he was lithe, his skin was dark like his uncle's, and his heavy hair, which was quite long for a boy's, waved in the breeze.

"Gosh, he looks a little like an Indian, a good one," Jim remarked.

"Will he mind if we go closer?"

"No, but I wouldn't pay too much attention to him," Mr. Fenton advised. "I'll go about my job and you amuse yourselves." He left them, and the boys proceeded to where the young farmer, or whatever he was, was engaged. They marveled at the speed with which he turned over the earth and before they were very close they saw that he was making some kind of trench. At the nearest end the work seemed to be finished, and then they could tell that he was making a terrace along the edge of the alfalfa plot. About half way down he had taken some very large rocks, fitted them with great nicety, filled in the crevices with smaller stones, filled in the space toward the hill with earth, and above the dark soil poked two rows of tiny green shoots of young corn.

"Gosh, he's planting as he gets the land ready. Great job, isn't it?" Bob whispered and his step-brother nodded. Presently they came up to the boy. When their shadows fell across his plow, he glanced up quickly and sprang back. They grinned cheerfully to let him know they were friendly, and Jim pointed to the new terrace.

"Fine," he declared.

The boy smiled, his eyes lost some of the terror which had leaped into them, and his body relaxed. He eyed them for a moment, then motioning with one hand, he led them back to the other side where he showed them a narrow trench. With one scoop of his shovel he removed the earth that still held the water as a dam, and it started to tumble through and race off toward the road, where it would be carried away into the lake. For several minutes they watched, and then they glanced at the useless bog.

"Cracky," Bob shouted with admiration. "Some irrigator. Look, it's draining off."

Sure enough, the long strip was getting dry around the edges, and promised to be emptied inside of an hour.

"If it stays dry, Uncle Norman will be tickled pink. Say, Jim, what do you suppose he is?"

"Search me," Jim responded.

"Seems as if I've got a kind of hazy idea of reading something about some old race or other using plows like that," Bob remarked.

"Me too. Maybe it was the Egyptians."

"Maybe, but holy hoofs, what's this kid doing it for?"

"As I said before, my esteemed step-brother, you are at liberty to search me thoroughly, but if you find anything, you have to let me in on it," Jim laughed. The boy watched them a few minutes longer, then picking up his tool, he hurried back to his work.

"You know, Jim, we thought this neck of the woods was going to be dull as ditch-water, but I've got a hunch that if we stick around we may be able to crowd some real excitement into our visit. I'm dying to know who this kid is and where he came from, mystery number one; I'd like to do some flying about Isle La Motte and perhaps we can see something that will solve mystery number two—what's happening to Uncle Norman's turkeys—"

"I'd like to do some observing and see if we can't get a line on that gang that is giving friend Bradshaw such deep furrows between his handsome eyes," Jim laughed.

"Me too, but gosh all hemlock, wouldn't Dad kid the life out of us if he knew we are out to help the little old world!"

"Not only Dad, but the whole shooting match on the ranch. Tell you what, Aunt Belle and Uncle Fent said we could stay as long as we like, and they meant it, even if we are boys. Let's organize a secret—s-e-c-r-e-t—mind you, detecting bureau, or what ever it is, and stay until we solve the three mysteries!" Bob proposed.

"I'm on. This end of the world doesn't look so bad to me. We'll let the folks know we're taking root for a while, the three of us, that includes Her Highness. We'll keep on the job until we win, or we have to admit we're licked." Bob held out his hand and the agreement was made, without further discussion.

"We'll have to explain to Her Highness," the younger boy declared.

"Sure thing. She'll be disappointed unless there's a lot of air work to it, and I have a hunch there will be."

"Oh, boys—"

"Yes Aunt Belle," Bob shouted.

"Do you know where your uncle is working?" Mrs. Fenton called from the roadway. "There's a telephone message for him."

"We'll find him for you," Jim promised. They hurried off in the direction Mr. Fenton had taken when he left them and soon the sound of a hammer ringing in the distance informed them they were on the right trail. A moment later they could see the man repairing a place in the rail fence that bounded the pasture.

"Uncle Norman, you're wanted on the telephone," Bob roared.

"All right, coming," the man waved, and dropping his work, came as fast as his long legs could carry him.

"Guess you're party's holding the line," Jim volunteered.

"They don't mind that around here," Mr. Fenton replied. He went ahead and the boys followed more leisurely.

"This certainly is a good looking spot. No wonder the early pioneers settled in rock-bound Vermont, but, gosh, what a fight they had to put up to get a living out of those rocks," Bob remarked as his eyes roamed admiringly over the green hills, across the blue water, on to the distant mountains.

"It isn't a rich state yet, but it has produced some fine men. Real rip-snorters, rearin' to go," Jim added. By that time they had reached the "hole" and could see the strange boy working industriously at his terrace.

"You know, Bob, we want to be kind of careful because we don't want to do any butting-in on that kid. Maybe, far as he's concerned, we had better mind our own business."

"Reckon you're right, but let's try to make friends with him," Bob suggested, and that was passed without a dissenting vote.

"Oh boys."

"Here," Bob shouted to his uncle.

"How long would it take you to get me to Burlington?" the man asked as he came up to them.

"Less than an hour," Bob answered.

"Would it be too much trouble for you to take me?"

"Not one bit," Jim assured him. "Ever been up in a plane, sir?"

"No, I haven't," the man admitted.

"Do you get dizzy easily, that is, does it make you sick to your stomach when you get on a high place and look over?"

"Oh no. I never get dizzy."

"That's all right then."

"We can strap you in," Bob offered.

"Will the plane carry three of us?" the man asked.

"Sure. There's an emergency seat in the back, and she'll carry some freight besides," Jim explained.

"Our dad didn't leave anything undone when he bought that plane, and besides, we helped in the selection. She'll do anything except herd sheep," Bob said proudly.

"We have parachutes and everything. Maybe you'd like to try one of them out," Jim offered.

"Not this time unless I have to," Mr. Fenton laughed. "A chap called me up on important business, and if I can get it attended to today, it will be a big help."

"Well then, get a heavy coat on. We have an extra helmet—"

"Shall I need rubbers?"

"If you intend to come down with the parachute over the lake," Bob answered.

"It's mighty nice of you—"

"We'll get Her Highness in ship shape."

"I'll be with you in five minutes," Mr. Fenton promised, and he was. He joined his young guests at the pier, Bob was already in the back, while Jim was fussing about the pilot's seat. Mr. Fenton was given the extra helmet and a pair of goggles, both of which he adjusted when he took his place after he had submitted to having the parachute and safety strap buckled properly.

"All O.K.?" Jim shouted finally. Mrs. Fenton had come down to see her husband start on his first flight, and she watched a bit nervously.

"I don't know about those contraptions, Norman," she said anxiously.

"They're great inventions, Belle. When we get rich, we'll have one," he promised her.

"I'd rather have a good horse and buggy," she retorted.

"A horse is all right, Aunt Belle. He never loses an engine or gets his wings ripped off," Bob shouted, then added. "All set in the rumble seat, Jim!"

"Right-you-are." Jim glanced at their passenger, assured himself that he was secure, then, opened her up, and they sped forward over the water, which was smooth as a sheet of glass. Mr. Fenton's lips moved, but whatever he said was lost in the roar of the motor. He grabbed the edge of the seat as Her Highness lifted her nose eagerly, and he hung on grimly as she spiraled in wide curves over the lake. At a thousand feet the young pilot leveled her off and they roared swiftly south toward the State's largest city. After about ten minutes, Mr. Fenton sat less rigidly. Jim picked up the speaking tube and handed the end to him, making motions how to use it.

"How do you like flying, Uncle Norman?" Mr. Fenton nodded and smiled. He didn't feel quite equal to carrying on a conversation yet. Jim followed the lake, and as they were approaching their destination, he spoke again to his passenger. "If we land on the water will that be all right for you, can you get to your place easily?"

"Yes, the office isn't far from the east shore." Mr. Fenton felt like an old timer now. He was thoroughly enjoying himself.

"Ten minutes more," Jim told him, and he nodded. Presently the pilot shut off the engine, and the man looked startled at the sudden silence. He glanced at Jim, who grinned reassuringly as he kicked the rudder about and brought Her Highness into a long glide toward the spot he had selected for the landing. The plane touched the water lightly, sped along a few yards and stopped beside a long pier.

"Are we here?" Mr. Fenton asked.

"Yes sir. How do you like air traveling?"

"It's wonderful, but I did almost get heart failure when the motor stopped," he admitted.

"Begun to wish you had brought your rubbers?"

"My rubbers and a boat."

"Is this place near enough?"

"Plenty." Jim helped him out of the straps, and by that time Bob stepped over the fuselage to give a hand.

"Glad you didn't try to jump over, Uncle Norman. How are your air-legs, wobbly?"

"A bit cramped." He stretched them both, found they would work, and in a moment he mounted the boat pier. "I don't expect to be more than half an hour."

"We'll wait here," Jim promised.

"Oh, look at the hydroplane," shouted a small boy on the shore.

"They are calling Her Highness names," Bob scowled.

"She's a hydroplane for the minute," Jim replied. "Let's taxi around the water."

"It's getting kind of rough. Up at North Hero it was as smooth as a sheet," Bob answered. "Wish I knew more about water and its tricks."

"I think we're going to have a blow," Jim speculated as Her Highness went rocking over the waves.

"There are some black clouds over south and west and they sure do look as if they are in a hurry. We'll have them on our tail as we go back. Got plenty of gas? I read that in some places Lake Champlain is three hundred feet deep, and it's wet clear to the bottom," said Bob.

"There's an extra tank besides what is in the bus. Guess I'll feed her up. Somehow, I think a nice Texas desert is pleasanter to land on than water." Jim busied himself with the task and Bob helped look things over.

"Why don't you go back above the shore?" he suggested.

"We have to land on the cove when we get home, so why switch gears. If there's time this evening, we might locate a place to land on the farm, but we'll have to ask your uncle about that or we'll be coming down on some field he's planted."

"O.K. with me."

"Whoooo boys," Mr. Fenton shouted from the pier where he was standing with a group of men and an army of small boys who had come to see the take off.

"An audience. Do your prettiest, Your Highness," Bob urged the plane as his step-brother brought it around in fancy style.

"It isn't every farmer who has a couple of pilots to bring him to town in a private plane, free of charge," one of the men joked.

"Certainly looks like the farmers are getting some relief," another added. "They are going up in the air about it."

"It's time we did something," Mr. Fenton responded. "Shall I get in now, Jim?"

"Sure." Bob gave him a hand, the straps were re-adjusted, and the younger boy crawled back to his seat, attached his own parachute, and was finally ready. By that time the shore was lined with spectators.

"All ready. Contact," Caldwell shouted. Jim opened the throttle, and they were off in a jiffy. They could see the people waving and cheering as they came about a few feet above the lake. Then Her Highness zoomed, high and handsome and the town was left behind.

Because of the rising wind the return trip was not so smooth. They ran into bumps and pockets, and the force of the approaching storm drove hard behind them, pushing them forward swiftly. Jim zoomed to ten thousand feet in an effort to get above the troubled air, but even at that altitude there was no improvement. Occasionally he took a second to glance at his passenger, but Mr. Fenton was facing it bravely, although his eyes showed that he was a bit anxious. The young pilot took the speaking tube, signaled to the boy in the back, and almost instantly there was a red flash on the dial board, which meant Bob was paying attention.

"Better put your cover over, old man."

"Got her up," came the answer. "I'm snug as a bug in a rug. Want to know the readings back here?"

"Yes." Bob read them off while Jim compared them with the records on his own control board, and when it was finished, he called.

"All correct."

"You covered up?" Bob demanded.

"Going to fix it now. So long. Meet you on the ice."

"You needn't. I'm not a skate," came the chuckling response. Then Jim drew the storm cover over the cock-pit, switched on extra lights, and the plane raced forward, guided entirely by compass, and the sensitive instruments which kept him fully informed as to how high they were and how fast they were going.

The coming of the storm suddenly hit them with a bang and the young fellow fought with the controls to keep Her Highness balanced.

Glancing through the tiny window he was startled to see that it was pitch dark, and he had to look at his watch to be sure that night was still several hours away.

"Some storm," he remarked to Mr. Fenton, who answered courageously.

"Lake Champlain is noted for them. They are pretty tempestuous at times and this looks like a rip-snorter."

III
THUNDERING WATERS

As the sturdy little plane tore along through the thick blackness a deluge of water hit her suddenly with such force it might have been a cloud burst and she staggered under the fury of the impact. She wobbled, side-slipped, twisted and dipped with the strength of the storm beating her mercilessly every inch of the way, and the gale at her tail spun her forward like a leaf torn from a branch. Above the roar of the engine and the shriek of the wind through the wires, came the threatening boom of the Lake as its mighty waves smashed against the rock-bound shore.

Tensely Jim sat, his eyes watching the dials in front of him, his hands and feet ready for instant action. It was a struggle to keep her righted and the boy zoomed her to fifteen thousand feet in an effort to get above the ceiling of the tempest. But he only climbed into greater trouble, and after a resounding crash of thunder, the sky was split in a thousand ways by flashes of forked lightning. Quickly he nosed her down, eyes on the directional compass, but keeping their course was out of the question. They were being blown miles out of the way and he hoped they would not go far enough east to land them somewhere in the mountains. He had not an instant to glance at his passenger, but once or twice his hand came in contact with Mr. Fenton, and the man was sitting braced for all he was worth. Another flash of lightning showed their faces, grim and white.

The rain continued to pelt them, and finally Jim calculated that they had traveled in a northerly direction. Allowing for the wind that had driven them steadily, he turned Her Highness' nose about in an effort to reach their destination, and the frail little air-craft was almost rolled over. In Jim's mind was a vision of Champlain and he debated the advisability of shifting the landing gears from the floats to the wheels, but he decided to keep the former in place. He knew so little about the country, and where it was safe to land. In the blackness which enveloped them he could not hope to come down without a very serious smash-up. With Bob in the back and Mr. Fenton beside him, it was too great a risk to take. Then he saw the man pick up the speaking-tube, so he prepared to listen.

"Anything I can do to help?" was the question. Jim shook his head.

"We ought to be near your place but I don't know where to go down. Is the water very rough?" he asked.

"Yes. The waves will be high and now they are driving from the southeast and will be hitting our side of the island. During a storm like this, boats have to be put under cover or they get beaten to splinters," Mr. Fenton answered.

"Thanks," said Jim. The prospect wasn't any too cheerful.

Although it was still raining, he shoved back the protecting cover and tried to peer through the darkness. He could hardly see his hand before his face, but he waited, until suddenly, an almost blinding flash of lightning revealed the world. Just ahead of them were farms and patches of thickly wooded sections. The boy saw small houses, their windows lighted as if it were late at night. Low growing things, vines and shrubs were bent to the ground. The trees bowed and groaned in the throes of the storm. Some of the branches, unable to withstand the strain, were being ripped off and hurled through space. Beneath the racing plane the black waters of Champlain were whipped into giant rollers, and along their edges white-caps foamed ghastly yellow in the weird light. It was all shut out in a fraction of a minute, and Jim zoomed higher to get out of harm's way.

"We're about five miles north of our place," Mr. Fenton told him, and the young fellow grinned with relief. It was some comfort to know where they were. Grimly he fought to bring Her Highness to face the storm. Feeding the engine all she could carry he battled to get south, but it was a hard struggle, like shoving against an immovable, impenetrable wall. It seemed as if the plane barely moved forward, but her propeller screwed valiantly, and slowly they gained against the wind, but it drove them east.

"Any rocks or islands near?" Jim asked.

"Gull Rock, two miles directly east, and Fisher's Island. That's a couple of miles long. If you can head into the southern point of our cove, that is protected somewhat from this wind and the water will not be so bad," the man explained.

"We'll try it. Do these storms last very long?"

"One never can tell. Sometimes they come and go in less than an hour, and very often they last much longer."

"Then there is no sense in trying to stay up until it beats itself out," Jim remarked. He couldn't say anything more. Another flash of light gave them a brief glimpse of the world but they seemed to be far over the water. Mr. Fenton leaned out to make observations, but was promptly forced back to his seat.

"Wow," he whistled.

"Better keep low," Jim advised. Then came a series of flashes, and Mr. Fenton managed to get their location straightened out.

"We're still a mile north and about half way across the lake," he volunteered. "I see Fisher's Point, the north end."

"Thanks."

Jim brought the plane about hard, raced her across, then shut off the engine just as a flash revealed the cove at the south end. The boy could see branches being tossed on the waves and hoped hard that none of them would cripple Her Highness when she dropped down. Another prayer he sent up fervently was that the space was wide enough for them to stop short of the rocks. They hit the water, rocked forward and up and down choppily, then stopped, just as someone came racing along the shore waving a lantern.

"Is that you, Norman?" It was Mrs. Fenton and she was so frightened that she could hardly speak. Her face showed white in the darkness and she gripped the light as if she would crush it.

"We're all present and accounted for, Belle," her husband answered quickly as he hastened to get loose from the straps.

"Hello everybody!" That was Bob who bobbed up in the back seat like a jack in the box. "So, this is London, and here we are!"

"Oh, I've been so terrified. I telephoned to Burlington when I saw the storm coming and they said that you had started. It—it's been just awful, awful." Mr. Fenton splashed through the water to reach her side.

"We're a bit damp, Belle, but otherwise perfectly fine."

"I knew you would all be killed—" she insisted.

"But we aren't," he assured her again. "Need any assistance, boys?"

"No. We can manage all right," Jim answered. The rain was coming down with less force and here and there through the darkness showed streaks of yellow light. The boys got Her Highness secured to the pier, and hurried to the house, where they found that Mrs. Fenton was getting out dry garments for them, and a cheery blaze crackled in the wide fireplace, while from the kitchen came the welcome fragrance of the evening meal. They grinned appreciatively at each other and climbed to their own room under the rafters where they changed their wet clothes. When they came down Mrs. Fenton was just putting out the lights because the darkness had lifted, as if by magic, and through the western windows they could see the glow of the evening sunshine.

"Well, what do you know about that!" Bob exclaimed, hardly able to believe the evidence of his own eyes.

"Have we been dreaming, or did we come back from Burlington in the teeth of a rip-snorting gale?" Jim demanded.

"It was no dream," Mrs. Fenton said fervently. "It was more like a nightmare. I was afraid to switch off the telephone because I expected every minute to get a call telling me that you had been wrecked on the Lake and were all drowned. And, I was afraid to leave the switch connected because I was sure the house would be struck by lightning. My, it wasn't a dream—not here anyway. Goodness, such a storm. I thought the house would be ripped from its foundations and come tumbling over my head. A tree was struck nearby for—oh, it did crash two different times—something awful. Land sakes alive, you boys must not go up again in such weather—goodness—"

The good lady stopped for breath and to pour glasses of milk out of a huge pitcher, while her husband served the rest of the meal. Mr. Fenton did not seem to have suffered any from his experience, and both boys considered the whole affair a most worth-while adventure.

"We've got some bus, Aunt Belle. Her Highness is the best in two countries. Have to say that because the shift landing gear was invented by an Englishman, but the rest is pure American," Bob smiled, then took such a long drink that when he looked up from his glass, there was a perfect white half-moon on his upper lip.

"You better shave," Jim suggested.

"Go on, shave yourself! How do you like air-traveling, Uncle Norman?"

"I think it's perfectly marvelous. Had no idea, really, how wonderful it is. When especially I think that I never, in all my Life, went so far and back in so short a time. We always take a full day to make the trip to Burlington, and today we made it in an afternoon."

"Were you frightened during the storm?" Jim asked.

"Have to admit that I was quite a bit nervous but when I saw you so cool and managing so easily, and how the plane responded to every move you made with those controls, why, I just naturally couldn't go on being a coward. It does not seem to me that Bob is over-stating the facts when he says the little plane is the best in two countries. I should say that she is the best in the world to come through such a grilling."

"Like to go up again?"

"I should indeed. Just think how automobiles and other modern inventions have placed us far ahead of my father's time. He had to use horses and oxen, and my grandfather did all his traveling, that is, any distance, on the lake-steamers. Sometimes it took weeks, and a storm such as we had this afternoon would have driven the boat into the nearest harbor to wait for fair weather."

"Gee," Bob said soberly. "How did those old boys ever get anywhere or have time to do anything?"

"When I was a boy I saw some of their primitive methods, Bob, but they did manage to accomplish a great deal."

"Some real nice day we'll give you a joy ride, Aunt Belle," Bob promised with a twinkle in his eyes. He fully expected that Mrs. Fenton would promptly decline such an invitation, but she looked at the men folk very thoughtfully, then a little pucker came between her eyes.

"Land sakes alive, Bob, you'll probably have to tie me fast and sit on me to keep me from jumping over-board, but I guess if you all think it's so fine, I can live through it. After I have the—er—joyous—I mean joyride, I'll write and tell your mother about it. She said that you took her up several times and now she wants her husband to get a plane."

"Right you are," Jim laughed heartily. "Mom's a good sport and so are you. We'll bind you hand and foot, and put weights on you, but I'll bet you will like it as much as Mom did."

"No doubt I shall," and Mrs. Fenton didn't smile over the prospect.

"Well, don't come down and ask me to buy you an air-plane, that is, unless the turkeys take a jump and we have a grand flock of them this fall, but it doesn't look now as if there is much chance," Mr. Fenton said. The last part of his statement was made soberly.

"Wonder how the boy's draining plan is working after that rain," Jim remarked as he recalled the work of the strange boy on the bog.

"When we finish supper, we'll go and have a look, but I expect the place is flooded way above the foot of the alfalfa bed," Mr. Fenton said.

"Now, how do you expect to eat your meal if you talk so much? Norman, you are not paying a bit of attention to those boys' plates and they are both empty."

"My plate may be empty, Aunt Belle, but my tummy is beginning to feel mighty content. I could purr," Bob told them.

"Well don't. It isn't polite at the table. You may roll over on the floor and kick your feet up if you like," Jim suggested.

"Don't you do anything of the kind," Aunt Belle said hastily. "The very idea. Is that what you do when you have a good meal at home?"

"No, Mom wouldn't stand that," Bob answered.

"We tried it once at school and it didn't go so well there either," Jim added gravely, and Mr. Fenton laughed heartily.

"How many demerits did they give you?" he asked.

"Ten apiece," Jim answered.

"And we had to average ninety-five on four subjects to shake them off," Bob added. "It's a cruel world."

"The world is a great little old place. It's only the people in it, I mean some of them, who make it unpleasant," Jim declared. "I can't eat another mouthful."

"This is my last," Bob announced regretfully as he swallowed the bite of cherry pie. "That is, I mean the last for the time being."

"All right, it's a good thing you added that because you are not at home now and you don't know where the pantry is located—"

"Don't kid yourself. I ascertained the location yesterday afternoon, before I'd been here twenty minutes."

"You would! Where was I?"

"Luxuriating in Champlain. I watched your fair form in the red bathing suit while I ate gingerbread and milk—"

"Humph, that's nothing, I had some when I came in—four pieces and two glasses—cream on top. Come along—that is—is there anything we can do to help you, sir?"

"No, thank you, Jim. I have a couple of chore boys and if you helped they might think I do not want them any more. We want you to enjoy your stay in Vermont—"

"Great guns, we are. It's a grand State even if we could put it into a comer of Texas," Bob replied sincerely.

"You ought to like it, your mother was brought up here, but goodness sakes, she went off when she wasn't much more than a girl. She was married right here in the parlor. I can remember it just as if it was yesterday, then the pair of them drove away in the two seater with old shoes tied to the end. They did look handsome. Your pa was all spruced up—and the next year they were in Texas—"

"You boys coming?"

"Yes sir."

As they went out onto the front piazza, the sun was setting and the sky was streaked with brilliant red and gold which shone magnificently through the trees. There was no doubting that the storm had been an actuality, for a deep stream was racing down the run-off toward the lake, and everywhere the place was strewn with leaves and branches that had been broken. The Rural Free Delivery Box was leaning wearily against a maple, as if the struggle to keep upright had been altogether too much. The three picked their way across the road with water dripping from trees and shrubs, and the ground soggy underfoot. They were soon past the garden, and at the further side they could see the foreign boy busy working, but this time his uncle was with him.

"Whoo-oo," Bob called cheerfully. The boy straightened up and smiled, then he came toward them and they went to the ditch he had showed them earlier in the day. It was full to the top with water which was running off as hard as it could go, and in spite of the storm there was little more water on the bog than had been there at noon time.

"Huh!" Mr. Fenton gave a little grunt of astonishment.

"Looks as if it's working all right, doesn't it?" Jim remarked.

"It certainly does. It'll be a great thing for me if he gets the place drained for that land is a piece of the best. Don't see how he's doing it. I had an expert engineer here to dry up that section and he couldn't accomplish a thing. Said the only way was to ditch it to the lake, then fill in the hole, use a lot of lime, like a concrete mixer and bring the hill forward. A mighty expensive job it would have been and then part of the land wouldn't be very good," Mr. Fenton explained.

"Reckon this boy is some sort of wizard. He's bewitching it," Jim suggested.

"Wish we knew something about him," Bob added.

"Don't blame you for being interested, Bob, but wc like to mind our own business around here. They seem to be honest and capable and don't interfere with what doesn't concern them—"

"Oh, we're not going to make blooming pests of ourselves, but we thought it would be fun to get acquainted with him. Wish he could speak English," Jim explained.

"I don't believe that he's spoken to anyone since they came. His uncle speaks fairly well. He seems upstanding. There isn't any harm in trying to make friends with the boy, but I wouldn't—"

"Butt-in? We won't unless he's willing to have us. Know what he reminds me of, Bob?"

"What?"

"Some of those Indians, the chiefs, you know the fellows that are so straight, clear-eyed, and sort of fine. He seems like that, only maybe an even better sort. The Indians we see now aren't so much like that."

"He is a little like that, but I don't believe he's an Indian. Maybe he's like they used to be a long time ago before the white men took all the pep out of them," Bob agreed.

"I don't know any Indians, but I never heard that they were very hard workers, not farmers I mean. It would be queer for one to be interested in that sort of thing. They like hunting—"

"Yes, that's right. Dad said a few of them made good cow punchers, but they never got much chance to show what they might do." Just then Corso came toward them. His face was grave but his eyes wore a pleased expression.

"It is good?" he said as he motioned toward the receding water.

"Very fine," Mr. Fenton answered heartily, then he added, "You must not let the boy work too hard. He does not look very strong. Why not have one of the men help him in what he is doing? I can get a chap who will do as he's directed, and this piece of work will be a great improvement to the property." Corso smiled.

"That would be so excellent," he agreed.

"All right. I'll have him here in the morning."

"He can the English speak?"

"Sure. You can talk to him, and I'll tell him I want him to follow any instructions you give him." Mr. Fenton was glad that Corso agreed to the plan for as the work promised to be a success he was anxious to get it finished as quickly as possible.

"We better look after Her Highness before it gets too late," Jim proposed to his step-brother.

"All right," Bob agreed, then turning to the boy, he grinned. "So long, Old Top!" The youngster frowned—

"Old Top," he repeated, "so long, Old Top."

IV
A MYSTERIOUS FIND

The next morning broke clear and beautiful as only a late spring day can start. The step-brothers found Aunt Belle busy canning rhubarb, and she eyed the two dozen jars with keen satisfaction.

"There, that's finished," she announced.

"Did you do all that this morning?" Jim asked for the sun was hardly well out of the Lake and was sending a golden path dancing across the water.

"Land o' Goodness, yes. Tomorrow I'm going to make some dandelion wine, and before sun-up is the best time of day to get work done, to my way of thinking," she replied as she bustled about getting the meal ready.

"Then suppose we give you that joy-ride right after breakfast," Jim proposed, and he looked at her to see if she had changed her mind.

"Land o' Goodness, you boys don't believe in giving a body a minute to worry over doing a thing like that. I don't know—"

"There's no time like the present," Bob teased her, and she smiled.

"I might's well get it over with and it will be a real experience. I can think of it all winter. All right." They both had a hunch that she was eager for the adventure, but she was mighty nervous about it, just the same. "It's kind of like going to have an operation or a tooth pulled," she told them and they laughed.

"You won't feel that way about it when you come back."

"Coming back will be a relief, like when the tooth or the appendix has been taken out. I suppose I'll be kind of shaky and queer, but the agony will be over. Now, you sit right down and help yourselves. Norman told me to be sure to wrap up warm." She hurried away and the boys grinned, then obeyed orders. By the time they had finished, Mrs. Fenton appeared, wrapped from head to foot almost like an

Eskimo. Her lips were set grimly and her fists were clenched for the ordeal.

"Now, don't you be afraid, Aunt Belle. It isn't any worse than sitting in a rocking chair, and it's much more exciting."

"I expect you're right. It was exciting watching you drop out of the sky on a streak of lightning yesterday," she gave a nervous giggle.

"We won't stay up very long, and if we see the tiniest cloud, we'll bring you right back," Jim promised.

Fifteen minutes later they were ready for the start. Aunt Belle had been given advice and instructions, strapped fast and parachuted in case of an emergency, her head encased in one of her nephew's helmets and goggles adjusted so she could pull them down. The speaking tube and field glasses were close at hand. This trip Jim was in the back seat while his step-brother was beside the passenger. Not a word did the lady utter during the preliminaries, but when young Austin called that all was as it should be in the rear, she braced herself stiffly, her frightened eyes searching the velvety-blue heavens for a sign of a cloud which might possibly spell danger.

"All set!" Bob shouted as he opened her for an easy take-off.

Her Highness seemed to realize the importance of behaving like a member of the royal family and did her part like a charm. She skimmed over the lake, circled widely, nosed up speculatively, lifted slowly on a long gradual climb, the motion of which was truly as pleasant as being rocked comfortably in a grandmother's big chair. Up they went five hundred feet and by that time they were beyond the south end of Fisher's Island and sailing gaily toward the narrows below the Point. Bob leveled off, they soared ahead, came partly around and climbed again at easy stages until the altimeter registered twelve hundred feet. The boy was glad that his aunt had asked no questions about the control board. Her Highness roared across North Hero Island, turned south again toward Grand Isle, then curved to come back. By that time Mrs. Fenton was wearing a very surprised look, and a moment later, she gave a relieved sigh, relaxed, and even sat up a little. Her lips moved and the boy knew that she was saying:

"My land o' goodness."

"Look," he pointed ahead and she followed the direction with interest, and after five minutes more, she was gazing over the side with fine unconcern. Then Bob pressed the glasses upon her, and she raised them to her eyes, and smiled at the wonders she beheld.

As Mrs. Fenton had never been "joy riding" before, the boys had agreed not to keep her up too long this first trip, so Bob brought Her Highness about, roared over the country his aunt knew; crossed the island above the bridge which connects North Hero with Isle La Motte, and curved over the latter stretch of land until they were sailing on a line with the turkey farm.

Jim in the back seat had time for observation, so he took a good look at the place. He had no difficulty in making out the ancient homestead, the old house where he guessed that Hezzy Burley, the poultry man, lived with his helpers. Close by were a number of hatcheries, and further along high wire-covered pens where turkeys, young and old, strutted timidly. The boy didn't have time to get a bird's-eye view of the whole farm, but he did notice that it came down to the lake on one side, and stretched back over a belt of timber and beyond a hill which looked as if it might be a very delightful place to ramble, but no good for landing a plane. As he glanced with interest at the Fenton property, he thought he saw some men in a ravine and decided they were hikers, or merely out for a stroll. Then, suddenly it occurred to him that they had no business on the property and it might be a good idea to tell Mr. Fenton and have Hezzy keep on the lookout for them. The boy wondered if the watch dogs had arrived, but his mental query was answered immediately, for he saw two dogs racing down to the water, and both of them plunged in for a swim. They looked like a very capable pair and he hoped they would be able to save Bob's uncle from having to mark off another bad year in his turkey business.

Her Highness was now soaring as gracefully as the white gulls they passed on the water, and Bob shut off the engine. The plane began a beautiful descent, and in a minute more she was floating toward the pier.

"Well, how's the tooth, Aunt Belle?" Bob teased.

"My land sakes alive, if it isn't the beatinest. There, I never slept a wink all night thinking about it, wishin' I'd been a better Christian in case I never got down to earth again, and all that worry—"

"Was a dead loss," Jim laughed.

"Yes it was," she admitted honestly. "It was just marvelous. Now, I've got to hurry. My fruit man comes through in a few minutes and I want some lemons. Tourists say this fruit wagon is kind of interesting and curious, maybe you boys would like to look at it," she invited. "It comes from Montreal, through the customs, and we can buy things cheaper than we can get them from our own stores. It seems queer, but it's so." They had unstrapped her and she smiled.

"I'd like to see him. We have some queer covered wagons that are driven through Texas. How did you like the ride?"

"A lot, and I'm ever so much obliged to you both. My land o'goodness—I mustn't forget to write to your mother and tell her I've been up with you. Her Highness is real pretty, isn't she!"

"We think she is," Bob answered with pride.

"You got a right to think that." Aunt Belle stood a moment to admire the plane, which did look particularly lovely as the sun shone on her broad wings, and the water beneath her, splashed gently about the floats. "She's a beauty."

"I saw some men, hikers I guess, back of your turkey farm," Jim volunteered as they went toward the house.

"There's a lot of people living at the north end of the Isle, and they are likely to go roaming all over the place. Sometimes the school teachers take nature classes to study the trees, and the Boy Scouts asked permission to camp there. Hezzy knows them all and he lets them go parts where they won't do any damage or scare the birds."

"Probably it's all right then." Jim dismissed the idea that he might have spotted something important, and followed the others into the house.

"I got some bananas, Mees Fenton." It was a soft pleasant voice that spoke, and the lips were parted in a wide smile.

"Little Greaser?" Bob said in an undertone.

"More likely little Canuck," Jim reminded him. "And he's not so little at that." The man was certainly picturesque in his baggy trousers, tied at the knees with pieces of new hemp, a red flannel shirt, and velvet jacket. He stood over six feet in his moccasins, which were of thick deer skin, and he might have been taller, but the weight of his hat must have kept him down.

"I'll be right out, Pedro," Mrs. Fenton called and she hurried away to rid herself of the extra clothing she had donned for the air ride. The two boys strolled out on the veranda to wait for her, and they could see the huge covered truck standing under the shade of two of the maples that edged the winding main road. Being sure of a customer, Pedro proceeded to his wagon, opened the end doors, leaped lightly over the tail board, and disappeared.

"Cracky, it doesn't look like any wagon I ever saw before," said Bob.

"No." They studied it with interest. It was heavily built, evidently constructed for long hauls and to carry heavy loads. The "cover" was of wood and metal, and the whole thing was painted a brilliant red and deep blue.

"Anyone would recognize that as far as he could see it," laughed Bob. "Oh, here you are." Mrs. Fenton came out with a basket on her arm and the three made their way to the caravan.

"Do all these peddlers have wagons like that?" Jim wanted to know.

"Good land, no, only Pedro. He had it made specially. Fills it up in Canada. He has to carry a great deal of truck to make it pay because some of the customs are high," she explained.

"Does he pick up American goods to take back?"

"Yes, and sometimes he does a little freighting when he can't buy our farm products." They had reached the end of the wagon, and the boys were amazed at its capacity. It seemed to hold a store full of goods. Besides the early vegetables, lemons, bananas, oranges, and pineapples, there were moccasins, Indian bows and arrows for youthful purchasers, bright blankets, and some skins hanging from the top. Mrs. Fenton looked over the wares, made her selection, and finally the transaction was completed. Pedro got a pail of water from the lake and gave his engine a drink, then climbed into the seat, waved cheerfully, and thundered colorfully off toward the next farm. In a minute he disappeared over the hill, but it took longer for the noise of his machine to diminish in the distance.

"Golly, he could take half the State over the border in that bus," Bob declared, then added as he saw the foreign boy coming from the garden, "Here's our friend. Hello," he called. The boy stopped, eyed them keenly, then smiled and showed a set of teeth so perfect that any dentist would have given half his kingdom to use his picture in an advertisement.

"Old Top, so long."

"Guess that will hold you for a while," Jim roared. "You are dismissed, my brother, Old Top."

"Aw I say, that's wrong. Hello!"

"Aw," the boy repeated—"Aw, hello."

"That's more like it." He pointed to his step-brother. "Jim." The boy looked at Jim, who flushed under the scrutiny. "Jim," Bob said again.

"Jimmm?"

"You got it. Jim."

"Aw, Old Top; Jim, so long; hello."

"Will you listen to the vocabulary. Ain't that marvelous!"

"It ain't," Jim scowled, then he pointed to Bob. "Bob," he explained. The boy seemed to understand that it was some sort of introduction.

"It ain't Bob?"

"Yes it is," Bob insisted, pointing to himself. "Bob."

"Bob? Jim?"

"Great," they both nodded gleefully. "You're a regular chatterbox."

The boy repeated the words he had learned and seemed to enjoy the sound of them. Then he stood a moment, straight as a young sapling, the expression on his face changed to a sober one, and into his deep, fine eyes, came a thoughtful look, which seemed to be habitual to them. As they met his gaze, any desire they might have had to have fun with him, disappeared, and the step-brothers felt a strong urge inside them to befriend this young foreigner.

"Bet my share of Her Highness against a plugged dime that he'd make a great pal," Jim remarked.

"I'm not taking you up. Let's see if we can't teach him more English. That won't be butting in," Bob proposed.

"Maybe we can do a little," Jim agreed. But just then a soft whistle came from further up the road and the boy turned quickly, leaped over the low fence and started toward the sound. The boys watched him until a moment later he joined his Uncle, who had evidently called. They both hurried in the direction of the lake, and a few minutes later, the young Americans heard the dip of oars as a boat was shoved off onto the water. Aimlessly Jim and Bob followed more slowly until they were standing on the shore, and they could see the boat skimming swiftly north.

"They parked it here. Guess they're going home to lunch, and it's easier than walking up the road," Jim suggested. He glanced at the marks on the rocks and sand where the boat had been left. Bob stared at the spot as if he expected to learn something of the two mysterious persons who had just left it.

"Here's a can, or something." Bob stooped and picked up a small covered box. It was somewhat the shape of a tobacco box such as men carry in their pockets, and was no more than an inch thick.

"That isn't tin. Maybe they dropped it," Jim said as he turned it over in his hand.

"Say, know what that looks like?"

"A box—"

"Sure, but the metal looks like my silver watch did—you remember it got almost coal-black—sort of brownish."

"So it does. Guess this is silver. We better keep it, and if it belongs to the kid, return it to him."

"Sure. If it doesn't belong to him, Aunt Belle may know who owns it. Mom said that in a little place like this everybody knows all about what everybody else owns." Jim turned the thing over in his hand again, gave it a little shake, and as he did so, the cover sprang back, as if he had pressed a concealed spring.

"Well, look here," he exclaimed. The two looked inside but all they could see was some bits of colored string. Carefully Jim took hold of one and gave a little pull.

"You'd better not do that. The string may be around something real small and you'll lose it," Bob suggested, but before the words were out of his mouth, the entire contents was in Jim's hand. "What do you make of that?"

"Maybe the kid has been trying to be a Boy Scout. It's nothing but colored strings full of knots, but it's a queer sort of string at that. I never saw anything like it—"

"You'd better put it back," Bob urged. "It isn't any good, but if the kid was having fun with it, we don't want to be goops—" Both boys turned quickly as they heard the sound of oars being plied swiftly as if someone were rowing in a great hurry. "He's coming back." Hastily Jim stuffed the odd looking string back into its container and snapped the lid shut.

"Wish I hadn't been such an inquisitive boob," he muttered. By that time the boy and his uncle had almost reached the spot, and both of them seemed to be anxious about something.

"Did you drop a little box here?" Bob called as the boy leaned on the oars to let the boat come ashore. Corso's face lighted with relief, as if the thing they had lost were of great value.

"Yes, sir," he answered.

"Well, that's good. We just picked it up." Jim stepped hastily forward and restored the find to its owners, but to his surprise, they both leaped out.

"Much sirs, we thank you." The man took Jim's hand, and to that pure young American's utter embarrassment, stooped and kissed it. Hastily he drew it back.

"Aw, that's all right," he said in confusion.

"Glad we saw it before the waves carried it off," Bob declared. He was congratulating himself that it was his step-brother who received the homage, but his delight was short-lived, for the boy took his hand and performed as did his uncle.

"Much thanks, Bob—Jim," he said chokily.

"Aw, it isn't anything to make a fuss over," Bob answered quickly, and his face flushed to the roots of his hair. In his heart he was glad that none of the cowpunchers from Cap Rock were there to witness such a display of gratitude.

"Much thanks," the uncle said again, and the two backed away.

"Don't mention it," Jim said hastily. "We have to go, or we'll be late for lunch. We would have given it to you this afternoon if you hadn't come for it." They both bowed low, then sprang into the boat and rowed off, but now their faces were wreathed in smiles and as the distance grew between them and the shore, they began a sort of chant which sounded like the wind sighing through the cedars.

"Come along, let's get a move on. I don't want to be kissed any more. Gosh, they must be French," Bob exclaimed, and the two started to run as if the Old Harry were after them. When they came in sight of the house, they stopped. "I'm not going to tell anyone about that box."

"Mum's the word. If we tell about finding it, we'll have to tell about giving it back. Perhaps it's some sort of heirloom, but it sure is a queer sort of thing to make such a fuss over."

"I'll say, maybe now that we gave it back, Corso and the boy will be friendly and we can ask them where they came from—"

"Maybe we can, but we're not going to be little interrogation points unless they give us the information without our asking for it. Dad says a gentleman recognizes another gentleman and they treat each other accordingly—"

"Well, that's O. K. with me," Bob nodded. "But I thought we might get an answer to one of the mysteries."

V
A DISCOVERY

"I have some errands at Isle La Motte station, boys, and I'm running up there in the car. If you'll condescend to ride in anything so slow and primitive, I'm driving down to the turkey farm and you can see what it looks like," Mr. Fenton invited that afternoon as the boys came up from a swim.

"Well, of course, sir, we wouldn't be so impolite as to say that we scorn to use your only mode of conveyance," Jim grinned broadly.

"But we'll accept with pleasure. I'm looking forward to meeting Hezzy and seeing his face when he learns we are members of the family," Bob added with relish.

"How soon are you starting?"

"As soon as you are ready," Mr. Fenton told them, so they raced into the house and made a wild scramble to get into their clothes. In record time they were out, their faces were flushed from the stampede and the cold dip.

"You surely have a grand lake in your back yard. I never enjoyed a swim so much in my life," Jim volunteered as they climbed into the seat of the waiting car.

"Suppose that you have water-holes in Texas and you boys fight over the swimming privileges just as the cattle men used to fight over keeping them for their stock," Mr. Fenton remarked.

"We don't kill each other."

"We're not so fond of a bath as all that, Uncle Norman. There are four creeks on the ranches, and one corner of Mom's takes in a slice of Pearl River."

"In the spring we have it to burn. Sometimes it fills the gullies and part way up the canyons, but that's only in the Cap Rock section. Almost at the edge of the cliff the land stretches away for about three hundred miles and that's pretty dry. Some of the ranchers drove wells, but they had to do it a dozen times before they had any luck, and most of them are driven more than a hundred feet to reach water. They force it to the surface and make pools," Jim explained.

"Is that for the cattle?" Mr. Fenton was greatly interested.

"Yes, and to irrigate the grain."

As he listened to the bits of description of the boys' home in Texas, Mr. Fenton was driving along the road which ran in a wavy line all the way around the Island and in ten minutes they came to the log bridge which led to Isle La Motte. Here and there they passed Vermonters who exchanged greetings with the farmer, and occasionally they passed touring cars. Some of them were carrying full loads, while others were less crowded. A good percentage were trying to take in all the beauty of the "Islands" they were crossing, but the rest looked bored and some of them read. The cars carried plates from almost every state in the Union and were everything from shiny and new, to rattly and very old.

"Great snakes," Jim remarked. "Looks as if the world and his wife have taken to their automobiles."

"Glad we have Her Highness. She can't be crowded off the road," Bob added and he glanced a bit disdainfully at the travelers. They drove across the bridge, hurried on north and at last came to the little depot, where Mr. Fenton took on a piece of freight, chattered a moment with the agent, then took his place again.

"Now, you'll see the farm. The place is one that Mrs. Fenton inherited from an uncle of hers. That end of Isle La Motte used to be rather thickly settled for these parts, but the old people died off and the younger ones went to other places to make their homes. It's quite a farm, nearly three hundred acres, but most of it is timber land, and it's too far from the main road to cultivate. If we didn't have the other place, we should have moved over, but it seemed ideal for a poultry farm. Vermont turkeys bring a big price, so we started in a small way and soon it was quite a success. The last couple of years haven't been so good. The birds are not easy to raise, and we expect many of them to die and don't mind if a few are stolen, but wholesale loss—a couple of hundred went two nights before you boys arrived."

"Cracky, that was a wollop," Bob whistled.

"Have many raids like that?" asked Jim. It sounded like the losses on a big stock ranch.

"There have been quite a few. Well, here we are." They drove up to the old house which had been built over a hundred years ago, but in spite of its great age, it was sturdy looking. Its architecture, doors, mullioned windows, and wide floorings in the "porch" would have gladdened the heart of a "Colonial" collector. The boys did not know this, of course, but they could appreciate that it was a great old place. Mr. Fenton honked, and in a moment the door was opened and Hezzy emerged.

"How are you, Burley? Dropped around to show the nephews from Texas what a turkey farm looks like." Hezzy came down the steps and the boys eyed him gravely. "Want you to meet the boys. Jim Austin and Bob Caldwell. They are going to spend a part of the summer with us."

"Pleased to—" Hezzy was beside the car now, his glasses resting low on his nose as he could look over them.

"Reckon Mr. Burley has met us before," Bob grinned.

"Oh yes, I forgot. They told me they landed with their plane on the cove and you drove them away. I explained the troubles you have been having."

"They didn't one of them say they come from your place, just landed on the lake and said they wanted to see the farm. That was two days, or less, since we lost that big batch—I wasn't taking no chances," Hezzy said quickly. He wasn't a very prepossessing man to look at, but now he smiled at his employer and was most affable.

"Sure, we understand," Bob assured him, but Jim said never a word.

"Want to look around now?" Hezzy invited cordially.

"We will. I haven't much time but they can get an idea and come back later if they want to see more," Mr. Fenton said as they climbed out of the car.

"Oh, they can see it in a few minutes," Hezzy answered. "It's pretty much all alike." He led the way toward the shore, and presently the three were going through the houses, past the wired run-ways, and to the larger enclosure where the bigger birds were confined.

"The thieves must have done some damage if they went over those wires," Jim remarked as he noted the fine mesh, and that smaller yards were enclosed like a box.

"They got in through the houses," Hezzy answered promptly. "At night."

"Got good locks?" Bob asked.

"Best we can buy," his uncle replied.

"Wish we could help you find the thieves," said Jim, "but we're kind of dubs. I lost my watch at school and tried detecting. Began to suspect the president, then I found it in my other suit pocket, so I swore off sleuthing."

"You bet, it's a dangerous business, but I suppose you have someone on the job, Uncle Norman!"

"Well, no, we haven't. We just try our best to catch them when they come for more, but we haven't been able to discover the thieves yet. I see that you have the watch dogs. Are they good?"

"They seem to be fine dogs, but one of them is sick this morning. I gave him a physic. It's the only thing I know to do for him, but I guess he'll come around," Hezzy told them.

"You'd better call up the veterinary. I paid a good price for those beasts and should not like to have to buy another pair," Mr. Fenton ordered.

"I called up the vet. He told me what to give him," Hezzy answered.

"Well, guess that's all you can do. Someone might try to poison them, so keep an eye on what they eat."

"I'm not taking any chances," Hezzy said hastily. "Want to have a look at him?"

"Not this afternoon, I want to get back. You boys seen enough to satisfy you for the time being?"

"Sure," Jim answered. "There isn't much to see. Sometime when you are coming again, we'll tag along if you'll let us, sir."

"Be glad to have you."

"Sure, bring them along any time," Hezzy spoke up. "I'm sorry you didn't say you belonged to the Fentons when you were here yesterday, but I didn't know, and turkeys are the scariest birds that grow wings."

"That's all right, but we thought you might have heard about the plane and recognize us from that," Jim told him.

"Fent told me you were coming from Texas in an airplane, but when a man's worried he don't stop to think. Only thing came into my head was you were some marauders and my men were both away for an hour."

"All right, come along." They made their way to the car and were soon on the way home.

"It's a great place, Uncle Norman. Maybe when we're flying around we can locate something which will solve the mystery for you, but you'd better not say anything to anyone because it might put the thieves wise and they'd work another way."

"Very well, I'll keep it under my hat, but don't either of you go taking any chances. I want to send you home with whole bones and not in sections. That would be a poor ending for your trip."

"We'll be careful. We were over the island with Aunt Belle this morning and I noticed the other end hasn't much good landing space. Too many trees and shrubs, except one hill that's kind of bare, but it isn't very big and it looks steep," Bob explained.

"Your aunt certainly did enjoy her ride," the man smiled.

"Don't we know it! We knew she would, but she was scared blue when we started—said it was like going to have a tooth drawn." By that time they were at home and after supper they took a stroll along the rocky beach.

"Got something on your mind besides your cap?" Bob asked his buddy.

"Yes, hair."

"The rest is vacant space—" Bob dodged a stone that his step-brother threw at him.

"No it isn't, you nut. Keep away from those trees or a squirrel will mistake you for a part of his supper," Jim retorted. They walked on a way in silence, then they came to a huge boulder, where the older boy sat down.

"I say, what are you thinking about? I never saw you still so long except when you're in Her Highness and her voice keeps you quiet."

"How did you like Hezzy?" Jim asked.

"Oh, he wasn't so bad when we were properly introduced. Guess if we had just lost two hundred turkeys we'd have been out with shot guns too. We'd have fired them first and sent apologies to the family afterwards. What do you think of him?"

"I don't know. It's giving me a brainstorm to find out. Can't blame a man for being on the war path under those conditions. He's probably the salt of the earth, as your aunt says, and honest as the day is long, but I can't get over the idea that if we met him on the range in Texas, we'd turn the bull loose on him," Jim laughed.

"Maybe we would," Bob admitted, then he grinned, "but you don't want to forget that you thought the president had your watch."

"Go on!"

"What's eating you besides the man's looks and his reception of us the other day?"

"Not much. It seemed to me that he wasn't overly anxious to have us come back—"

"Why yes he was—said to come—"

"Any time with your uncle. But when Mr. Fenton said we could come by ourselves and take a look, he said 'we could see it all in a few minutes.' Like as not, I'm barking up the wrong tree. Let's go up early in the morning and see what we can see around the border. I'd kind of like to talk with Bradshaw again. He was really decent and I'd like to know if he located any of that gang yet," Jim proposed.

"Suits me right down to the ground."

"We've been kind of grounded since we came. Suppose your aunt would mind letting us take a lunch to eat in the air, or some nice place we pick out?"

"Of course she won't mind. What sort of crab do you think she is?"

"No sort of crab, unless there is a very generous, likable variety, but we don't want to make extra trouble for her. Your mother said that the farm takes a lot of work and she has no end of things to do. Tomorrow she's going to can some more—"

"And she'll be glad to have us out of the way for a while." Bob was quite positive, and although his aunt showed no desire to be rid of her two guests, she was perfectly willing to fix them up a picnic lunch and by the weight of the basket she handed her nephew the next morning, it promised to be a bountiful meal.

"You boys be careful and if it gets stormy you'd better come right home. I'd be really worried—"

"You must not do that. Didn't we slide down on the lightning the other day?" Bob demanded.

"Yes, I know you did—"

"And didn't you enjoy air traveling?"

"Yes, yes indeed I did, I wrote to your mother last night—"

"Then don't waste any good worries about us," Bob grinned. "We'll be fine and come home to roost, like chickens."

"Hurry up, Her Highness is raring to go," Jim shouted. He was already in the cock-pit, and his pal raced to join him.

"All O.K.?"

"Sure Mike." Bob took his place beside his step-brother, adjusted himself, and in a minute Jim opened the throttle, the engine bellowed a challenge to the world, or a joyous roar that it was about to do something worth watching. Up they climbed a thousand feet, circled above North Hero, and as Bob glanced over the side, he caught glimpses of children and farmer folk staring at them. He waved gaily, then Her Highness leveled off and shot northwest.

"Going to have a look about Isle La Motte?" Bob asked through the speaking tube.

"No. If the thief is there I want him to think that we are not interested in looking for him," Jim answered, then added. "I'm more interested in seeing if we can find Bradshaw."

"Any special reason?"

"Not one." Jim answered emphatically.

They sped toward the boundary and both boys were filled with delight at being in the air. Bob kept the glasses to his eyes and every once in a while would point out something attractive so his step-brother would miss none of the delights of the trip. Jim did not wish to go straight north, so he bore westward, following the American side of the border and after an hour, circled about and returned pretty much along the same course. Once they saw a passenger plane soaring majestically south, and then they spied the mail-pilot racing toward them, so they went to meet him. The young fellow in the cock-pit eyed them for a moment but when they grinned and waved, he waggled his wings as a return salute. He seemed such a jolly sort that Jim came about and taxied along beside him for a while, then with a farewell wave, he spiraled high and circled away, the U. S. plane thundering toward Montreal.

"We ought to locate Bradshaw soon," Bob remarked as they were nearing the territory which their Mounty friend patrolled, and Jim nodded. The younger boy searched the rolling globe beneath them. Through the glasses he could see tiny homesteads, miles of unsettled stretches broken only by a rough road, and an occasional traveler scooting along in a car or seeming to crawl behind a team of horses.

"The place we picked up Bradshaw is about a mile ahead," Jim remarked, and this time Bob nodded assent. He paid even greater attention to his observations, and once he picked up something that puzzled him. It was a wooded ravine, the sides of which rose steeply and were bristling with overhanging rock. The boy guessed that it was the bed of a stream, but the water had either dried up or been diverted through another outlet. He followed its winding course, and calculated that it must be several miles long and extended well across the borders into the two countries. Twice he thought he saw something moving about, then he looked more sharply for he thought it might be a bear. In a moment more he discovered that it was a man, two of them in fact and they were making their way warily as if anxious to escape detection.

"Slow up a bit Buddy and zig-zag. I want to see this place." Jim nodded, reduced the speed, zoomed high and spiraled as if he were reaching for the ceiling, then dropped, and all the while Bob kept his eyes on that deep ravine.

"Spot anything, Buddy?"

"I don't know. You have a look, but be careful. Wouldn't that ravine down there be a corker place for bootleggers or smugglers to go sneaking from one side to the other? I see some men there now. What do you think?" Jim was already scrutinizing the place.

"Yes it would, but it's too big for the patrol men to have overlooked," Jim answered. "That old road runs pretty close to it. Law-breakers would keep out of a place like that."

"They might not just because it looks so inviting. They might figure they could get away with it because it's so easy, and they'd have it fixed up. See those fellows?" Jim nodded, and by that time he was keenly interested. He not only saw the two men, but further along he picked up two more who seemed to be hiding in the underbrush, and not far away he espied a two-wheel cart, which was painted green.

"Great guns, we've got to find Bradshaw and tell him. He may give us the ha-ha, but just the same, that's no ordinary bunch down there, and the men are not even smoking cigarettes. Here." He handed the glasses back to the younger boy. "Be careful no one notices that you are watching them," he warned tensely. He kicked the rudder, shot Her Highness' nose into the air, zoomed higher, and five minutes later, Bob caught his arm and nodded toward the land.

"Bradshaw is down there on the road! He's about five miles, I guess, from where I first saw that ravine, and it ends just a little way below him. Two fellows crawled up after he had passed, got on horses and separated, and Jim, they are following the Mounty, one on each side, as if they are watching him. They are just jogging along as if they are on old plugs, and Jim—there, oh gosh, there are two more coming out a mile ahead on the road." Bob was so excited that he could hardly speak steadily.

"Are they laying for him?" Jim asked tensely.

"I think they are. Come on, do something, and do it quick, for they are all trotting in close. I think he hears the ones behind, because he's turning around—Jim—" Jim looked over the side, and just ahead he could see the drama being enacted two-thousand feet beneath him.

"Hang on to your teeth," he roared.

With a swift flop he turned Her Highness' nose toward the earth, and with the engine bellowing he came tearing out of the sky. After the first second he shut off the motor, made it cough and sputter, and the plane began to spin and twist, tail first, then nose first. Both boys tried to watch what was taking place beneath them, and Jim's heart almost stopped beating as he saw that the Mounty was concentrating his whole attention on them. Even Pat had his eyes upward at the startling spectacle of a gyrating airplane that promised to be kindling wood in a few seconds. On they raced, and as they came, Austin saw that two of the outlaws were galloping swiftly, rifles on their arms, toward their prey. They seemed to have thrown caution to the winds and were taking advantage of the commotion above them to complete their wicked crime.

Bob clutched his step-brother's arm as he too took in the scene, but Jim was not unmindful of their own danger and one eye was on the altitude meter. At five hundred feet he took the controls, started the engine and lifted Her Highness' nose, then went on into a glide that brought them, a moment later, to a scant two feet of the snorting Patrick and the indignant Mounty. But before the man could utter a protest, Jim bellowed defiantly.

"Aw yes, suppose you think you own the air, and you're going to give us a blowing up. Well, come on and do it."

"I surely will," Bradshaw responded. He was surprised at the whole performance, leaped from his horse, and strode close to them.

"Well, go on and search me if you want to, you half-baked nut—"

"I say, how do you get that way?" Jim was out of the cock-pit, his arms raised above his head as if he were being held up.

"Go on and search," he shouted. "I'm not afraid of the whole Canadian army," then he added in a lower tone. "Search me and make out you're mad as blazes. Rip us both up loud and handsome. We saw some guys out to do you, and they are not far away. Savvy?"

"Yes, I'll search you, you rough necks." Swiftly his hands went over the boy from head to foot, while Jim alternated between bitter abuse, punctuated with bits of their story told in a lower tone. In the middle of the performance, Bob hopped out beside his step-brother.

"What do you think you're doing?" he yelled, and added, "Get out your gun, they're just back in some brush." The business-like automatic was instantly in Bradshaw's hand and he whirled on Caldwell.

"You quit shooting off your mouth," he ordered in fine style. "How did you chaps discover this bunch?" in a lower tone of voice. He began the search of Caldwell, and as the three stood they could see on all sides of them in case the outlaws decided to take a hand.

"We were looking for you," Bob answered while the man went through his breast pockets. "Saw a ravine back there with a lot of men in it. Looked queer so we came to give you the message, then as soon as we spotted you, we saw the bunch, four of them, closing in, so we did our little stuff with Her Highness. Now don't go taking anything that doesn't belong to you," he ended with a savage roar as Bradshaw drew a notebook out of his pocket.

VI

A CAPTURE

They stood in rather close formation, Bob and the Mounty facing each other, Jim so that he could observe anything approaching by either of two other points of the compass, and Bradshaw scowling fiercely and thumbing young Caldwell's book.

"You've got to explain this," he thundered.

"It's nothing but school reports, tests and names of classmates. You needn't go cribbing it," Bob growled angrily.

"What you American kids doing here anyway? Got a permit a fly into Canada?" Bradshaw demanded, but his eyes were narrowed as he focused them on the surrounding brush, his gun in hand. Suddenly he whipped it up almost to Bob's ear, and snapped:

"Come out of that you fellow."

Then followed a snarling curse, a smashing through underbrush, and the sharp crack of the automatic. Like a panther Bradshaw leaped forward and in an instant he dragged forth one of the pair who had come to head him off, but galloping hoofs and wild oaths proclaimed the departure of the other three. A moment later there wasn't a sound of them. The Mounty snapped handcuffs on his captive, trussed his feet, and shoved him along out of earshot.

"Pat," he called and the big horse trotted to his side. "Don't let him move." Pat promptly stepped over the man, who howled in terror, and lightly planted one hoof on his coat, pinning him securely.

"Some horse," Bob whispered with admiration.

"Now, you fellows give an account of yourselves. How did you happen to come down right here just as those lads were getting funny?" He spoke so sharply that the younger boy was sure the man believed they were a party to the hold-up, but Jim merely scowled back.

"Aw you ground hog. Our motor stalled up there and I couldn't get it going until we almost smashed. Can you understand that?"

"It's clear enough. What are you smuggling in that car?" He gave a little nod and strode with a determined tread to Her Highness.

"Not a blamed thing that doesn't belong to us," Jim shouted as he followed close.

"No?" Bradshaw leaned over as if to make a thorough inspection. "What's in the basket. A book of bed-time stories?"

"Grub," Jim answered sharply, then added. "And some apples for Pat."

"Thanks," the Mounty grinned. "Now, tell me, is that ravine the one that comes along like a letter S, deep and steep on both sides almost all the way. It ends in a rock cliff about a half mile below here?"

"That's it," Bob whispered and he sighed with relief as he realized that the officer had been playing the game.

"Great guns, we've had that under inspection, but we'll take another look into it. Do you know that out-post right on the line?"

"Sure. Has the two flags."

"That's it. My head chief is there now. I wish you'd fly over it and drop him a message—"

"We can give it to him," Jim offered.

"Don't want you to come down. We've been bluffing that I don't know you and it may help. Anyway it won't get you into trouble if any of the gang should see you again. I'll have to get this fellow locked up and make a report. I'm no end obliged to you. If you hadn't been on the look-out I might have had a nasty fight all by my lonesome. Wish you'd get away as soon as you can and drop this to my chief. You did me a mighty good turn and the department will appreciate your further service. Weight it down with these rocks, if you haven't anything better. I picked them up when I was cuffing our friend over there."

"Glad to. We'll keep a look-out from the air and you watch us. If we see any more surprise parties coming your way, we'll do a tail spin," Jim said softly.

"Thanks, but I fancy those fellows are willing to call it a day. Don't know why I've been picked out to bump off, but they may be planning to pull something in my territory during this beat. I'll be moving." He raised his voice and handed the note to Jim, then began in a louder tone. "Sure, I suppose your father is the President of the United States, but you beat it back over your own line and if you don't you'll wish he had the power of triplets."

"Aw," growled Jim.

"Smoke bomb," Bob added with relish as the throttle was opened and Her Highness got under way.

Further pleasantries were cut off by the thundering of the motors but the younger boy leaned over ostensibly to make faces at the officer, while his eyes searched the vicinity. He saw Pat still penning the captive to the earth, but not a glimpse did he get of another human being in the neighborhood. The plane zoomed a thousand feet, leveled off and headed for the Post the boys had seen a few days before. Jim had the stones, which he wrapped with the paper in his handkerchief, and then he knotted the note inside.

"All quiet on the front?" he asked his step-brother.

"As a mid-summer night's dream," Bob replied, then added. "I see the post, Buddy." Jim nodded for he too had picked it out and already Her Highness was gliding to a lower level. Down she rode swiftly, until she was only five hundred feet in the air, then they noticed the man-on-post come out, and level his glasses upon them. Jim raised his arm, and at the right moment he dropped the message over the side, and brought the plane about in a half circle, while they both watched the thing, the corners of the handkerchief standing out like a pair of rabbit's ears as it tumbled to the earth.

"He's got it," Bob shouted gleefully. A second man had come out of the hut and the boys saw them inspecting the present they had received so unexpectedly. The first man waved his hand and ducked into the house, and the boys, quite satisfied with the morning's work, grinned at each other.

"I'm empty, Buddy," Jim announced as they sailed off. The boys took a route almost straight west, and in half an hour they were above a rugged region which the map informed them was in the State of New York. They selected a plateau with little timber and some kind of stream. They glided to the landing place, and presently Her Highness was standing like a great wild bird, poised on the hill. The boys hopped out of the cockpit, looked about to make sure that there were no warnings posted to keep off the premises, then out came the basket.

"Want to build a fire and toast some of these marshmallows?" Bob proposed as he glanced at the food.

"Sure thing," Jim agreed readily. He got busy and cleared a rock while Bob gathered some bits of wood. In a few minutes they had the blaze crackling cheerily, and then they prepared to enjoy themselves thoroughly. Mrs. Fenton had put in almost a loaf of home made bread and butter sandwiches, a glass of plum jelly, six deviled eggs, slices of roast ham, olives, pickles, ginger cookies, milk, chocolate cake and candy.

"If we eat all this Her Highness will never be able to take us up," Bob grinned broadly as the things were set forth on the huge napkin.

"Intend to eat sparingly?" Jim inquired.

"Not so that you could notice it," Bob assured him. "When I come to think of it, I don't know where you're going to get any. I am hollow in both legs."

"I know what I'm going to do," Jim retorted promptly. "Pitch right in and if you get more than a toe full, you'll be lucky." With that threat, they fell to and ate with keen appetites, and when Bob finally stretched himself out on the rock with a huge sigh of contentment, the food was almost all gone.

"Gosh, I feel great."

"I'm right with you, Buddy," Jim answered. He lay on his tummy and for a few minutes they watched the tiny coil of smoke that rose in a wavering line from the fire, which was burning low. Austin did manage to throw on a few more sticks, that caught quickly, and crackled at a lively rate.

"Wonder what Bradshaw and his gang have been doing while we tanked up," Bob remarked. "Wish we could have been in on the scrap."

"Wish we could, but we might have been in the way. If we had hung around that ravine waiting for the fireworks, the chaps who were parked there might have been warned and that would have spoiled the show," Jim replied.

"Oh sure. By the noise they made, those chaps getting away may not have heard our little play. Reckon, they beat it to their headquarters to tell the other fellows. Seeing us again would have queered the party for the Mounties," Bob agreed.

"Yes, a plane is sort of conspicuous. Bet that message told the Chief, whoever he is, to surround the ravine and get the outlaws while the getting promised to be good."

"I saw one of those fellows pull out his gun. Gosh, they would have got Bradshaw if he had come riding right into their arms."

"It would have been some scrap, you bet. Bradshaw's no slouch."

"Not a bit. Wish he could come and see us at Cap Rock. Say, with Pat to help him, he's better off than if he were twins, or two policemen," Bob laughed as he thought of the efficient pony. "Some horse. Glad he's got a good master."

"You bet." They rested comfortably, and at last Jim broke the silence again. "Gosh, Buddy, remember that story of the brothers who watched the smoke go up the chimney?"

"Surely. I was just thinking about them. The Montgolfier boys. They were watching the fire and the smoke go up the chimney, and that set their brains to working and they wondered why the smoke went up. Queer isn't it when you think that a little thing like that happening around one hundred and thirty years ago, should develop into air travel!" Bob glanced toward Her Highness affectionately.

"She doesn't look much like the paper bags they made their first experiments with, does she?"

"I'll say she doesn't, nor the balloons that came a few years later. Gosh, I'm glad we don't live at a time when people were so ignorant that they thought everything new was a devil of some kind," Bob replied.

"We'd be in a nice fix if we got shot at or stabbed with pitch forks every time we came down. But, even at that, Jim, there are places in the world where the people are mighty savage. Dad says in some of the South American provinces they've never been able to conquer all the tribes, or civilize them. They are almost the same as they were when Columbus landed, and will fill a chauffeur full of poison arrows if they see a car driving through their land."

"Great horns. I'd like to go sailing over some of those places some time. Lindbergh must have seen some mighty interesting places when he went cutting air-paths over Mexico."

"He sure did. And isn't he the grand lad for keeping his eyes open and his wits about him?" Keen admiration for the Lone Eagle silenced them for a while, then Bob reached out and took a triangle of chocolate cake.

"I'll divvy up."

"You needn't." Jim made himself another sandwich. "Don't know where my lunch is disappearing, but I find I have a little vacant space which needs fueling." At that they both sat up, made a second attack on the food, but finally were compelled to stop.

"We may as well be soaring along," Jim proposed.

"Let's go over Canada and see if we can see any of the smoke from the ravine," Bob suggested eagerly.

"All right. You want to drive?"

"You bet, and you watch for the scrap." They packed the remains of the food in the basket, stored it into the cock-pit, poured water over the embers of their fire and cleaned the spot with a piece of dry pine brush, then gave Her Highness an inspection.

"Great old bird," Bob chuckled when they were sure that all was well. "She did a good job this morning." He took his place and Jim occupied the passenger seat prepared to be the observer.

A moment later Her Highness ran along the plateau, lifted her nose into the air, then climbed for all she was worth while Jim examined the earth beneath them. There wasn't a cloud in the sky, and the roar of the engine was a startling contrast to the calm forest they had just left. Caldwell watched his controls as they raced at three thousand foot height. Jim thoroughly enjoyed the inspection and occasionally made a note of something especially interesting, and often called his buddy's attention to the rolling globe. In less than an hour they were over the post where they had dropped the message, but if anyone was inside the shack, they did not come out to examine them. Then Bob turned sharply north, and soon they were about ten miles beyond the edge of the ravine and the place where they had stopped the Mounty.

"Slack up a bit and go south," Jim suggested through the speaking tube.

"All right," Bob agreed. He kicked the rudder, Her Highness circled, proceeded at a slower speed, and presently the spot in which they were so keenly interested, jumped into the lenses. At first glance it was as deserted as before, then Jim saw a coil of smoke rolling up into the wind. Concentrating with all his attention, he saw that some sort of shack was on fire, and just below the burning building, was a blackened spot that had been swept bare by the blaze. A couple of puffs snapped out from down the ravine, and a volley of answering shots spat viciously from the other end.

"The fight's still on, Buddy," Jim bellowed, and Bob looked over the side. They were getting close enough now so that they could see the battle fairly clearly, and they watched with tense interest. At one end they made out the Canadian policemen closing in on the desperadoes, who seemed to be sliding back behind a screen of brush they had dug up, and just a few feet from them the wall of the ravine rose sharply cutting off their escape.

"They'll have them in a minute," Bob exclaimed excitedly. "Suppose they can climb up that wall?"

"It looks pretty jagged to me, like tiers of boulders, but, zowee—if they do get up, there's a line of blue-coats waiting for them," Jim announced, and he would have danced up and down with joy, if he hadn't been strapped securely to the seat. Bob paid strict attention to his business, then, as the attack was started, he decided it would be no harm to circle about and see the finish of the fight. He knew that his brother would be in accord with the plan, so he proceeded to carry it out. He zoomed higher, kicked the rudder, raced the engine and was soon pounding at three thousand feet, where he leveled off for the ring, and started to fly so they had a grand view of the drama below. Jim kept his glasses fixed on the gully, and as the position of Her Highness was changed, he had a superior view of both sides of the maneuvers. Suddenly the wall that cut off the criminals was directly in front of his gaze and he began to wonder about it. It seemed strange that men who were probably accustomed to protecting themselves and taking every precaution, should select a place where they could be so easily trapped.

"The Mounties must have given them a special surprise," he remarked to himself, but just the same, that did not seem entirely possible. It seemed to the boy that there must be a gang who used the ravine as a hangout, a means of slipping into the United States or Canada whenever they wanted to, and they would need quite a force of men in order to keep themselves well posted on the habits of the men who patrolled the location. Then it occurred to Jim that the outlaws might not have used the place long and had not had time to prepare hasty exits. But that idea as it flashed through his brain did not seem at all plausible.

The boy remembered that Bradshaw had said the "gang" had been particularly successful in putting over every one of their schemes. That meant they were taking no chances, and surely they would none of them let themselves be backed against a high cliff where they were sure to be picked off with the rifles of the Mounties if they tried to scale it, and run into the arms of other officers if they did manage to reach the top. He studied the group of men firing furiously from behind the brush pile and rocks, then he wondered why the men on top did not fire down at them. That was soon answered, for he saw that the edge was steep and soft, and even as he watched, he saw a man slip. His companion grabbed him by the arm and saved him from going over into the ravine. The slip dislodged a quantity of gravel and brush which slid down behind the desperadoes. Two of them instantly whirled about ready to fire in case they were attacked from the rear. There still remained a few rods to be traversed before they would reach the cliff, and another man glanced up at the plane and shook his fist.

"Shouldn't like to kill any of them, but I wish we had a few tear bombs, or some little thing like that to put them out of business," Jim lamented. He couldn't help feeling that although it looked as if the officers would soon get their men, they must have some cards still up their sleeves.

"Say, Buddy," Bob bellowed, "There comes Pedro's covered wagon." He pointed, and although Jim could not catch the words, he followed the direction and had no difficulty in picking out the highly colored truck which was moving forward slowly along a road that looked as if it was used very little. It was about a mile from the ravine in an especially isolated section and Jim's eyes swept the vicinity as he thought that the huckster must be nearing his own home, but there wasn't a house for miles, and as near as the boy could make out, the road meandered along and finally slowed down near a dilapidated old rail fence which might mark an ancient boundary, or surround a pasture. Rocks and brush were piled above it, and as the boy looked, he saw that the truck stopped.

"Perhaps the old guy has heard the shooting," he thought, but if Pedro did, he gave no sign of either assisting or investigating. Instead he dismounted with agility, with some sort of huge bundle in his arms, and in a moment he was standing on the rim of the wagon bed. It took but a moment for Jim to realize that the man was throwing a canvas of dark green material over the brilliant truck.

"Bob, look," he bellowed. His step-brother, who had been giving his attention to the plane, glanced over and ahead, and his lips pursed up in a long drawn out whistle. By this time, which was really only a few minutes, Her Highness had passed over the end of the ravine, so Bob zoomed again, banked, and came about. He didn't propose to miss anything. In that brief interval, the red and blue truck had been turned into a green one so like the forest surrounding it that it could hardly be picked out. Jim saw Pedro take his seat again, then move forward a way until he reached a wide spot where he turned around.

"That old boy isn't all he pretends to be," the boy muttered. He would have liked to watch the "old boy" but he wanted to know what was going on in the ravine. He saw that the bandits were stretched in rows, only two men in the one nearest the blazing shack, while the Mounties were making their way forward cautiously. As Jim watched, he saw the rear row of outlaws slide swiftly back, then one of them disappeared under a rock. Another followed quickly, while the men in front continued to fire rapidly, as if to cover the fact that there were fewer men at the guns.

"Great Caesar's ghost. They've got an outlet there and are going to get away under the ground," Jim shouted, but he couldn't make Bob hear and he didn't want to take his eyes off the event even for an instant. Quickly he swept the country-side for a cave entrance, and then, in a moment, he picked it up. A man emerged stealthily, raced through the woods, and came out close to Pedro and his camouflaged truck.

"By gum and thunder," Jim exploded.

VII
A TAIL SPIN

"Buddy," Jim screamed as he clutched Bob by the collar. "They're going to get away." Bob looked over the side to see what it was all about, and in a moment he gave a grunt.

"Huh!" Caldwell took in the scene, then for a second he stared at his step-brother, mechanically bringing Her Highness around in a half circle. Then Jim had an idea. He pulled his note book from his pocket, fished out a pencil, and began to scribble hastily. When he had finished, Bob read the message.

'They are crawling away under the hill and there's a truck, Pedro's, but it's got a green cover, and is on an old road to the west, picking them up.

The Flying Buddies.'

Caldwell grinned at the signature, and he was already guiding the plane toward the Mounties, who were still peppering the cliff with their rifles. A few of them on both sides were edging up through the brush, but they were not firing, and the boys guessed that they expected to close in on the bandits, feeling sure the men could not escape. Jim glanced about for a weight, but the only thing was the lunch basket, so he caught it up, saw that the cover was secure, then tied the note on the handle with his handkerchief so that it could be easily seen.

"Shoot," Bob shouted when he was just enough below the Canadians to allow the thing to fall close by them and not force a man to expose himself to the guns at the further end.

The basket went over swiftly, spun around, tipped and tossed, and they saw it land. A man secured it without difficulty and waved an acknowledgment, while two others read the message. The boys couldn't see what action they took, nor did they hear the shrill blast of a whistle signaling to men stationed above the ravine. Bob brought Her Highness about, and sent her over so they could get a good look at the scene in the woods. While they watched, two men slipped across the road and jumped into the back of the huge fruit truck, which was moving slowly. Caldwell clenched his fists as he realized that the fellows would surely slip through the officers' fingers and he looked at Jim, hoping that his step-brother would have another idea, but Austin shrugged his shoulders. With anxious eyes Bob scanned the road. He noticed that the truck was nearing a point which was high and narrow. On either side rain and winter storms had dug deep gullies, leaving barely room for one vehicle of any kind to traverse it in safety.

Glancing at the altimeter, Bob read that the plane was less than a thousand feet up, so he banked, tipped Her Highness' nose, and zoomed in a swift, steep climb. The needle pointed to twelve hundred, fifteen, eighteen, but Caldwell held her throttle wide open, going full blast and climbing at top speed. The wind shrieked through the wires and threatened to rip the wings from the fuselage, but the pilot did not stop until he was thirty-five hundred feet and some distance behind the truck. Then he leveled off and the drama beneath them looked as if it were being performed by moving dots and dashes. The plane was brought about with a protesting howl, as Caldwell looked at the globe with its tiny specks, the narrow, treacherous road and wee puffs of smoke. He made a swift calculation, came to a decision, and shut off the motor.

The sudden silence was punctuated by faint booms of the guns cracking far below, and Jim looked inquiringly at his step-brother, who was sitting calmly, but flushed as Her Highness' tail dropped; nose tipped foremost, then began to spin slowly, held up by the force of the wind from underneath, carried forward like a leaf caught in the breeze, and irresistibly drawn down by the laws of gravitation.

Jim hadn't the faintest idea what his step-brother hoped to gain by the reckless maneuver, but he saw that Bob had some sort of plan, and that every fibre of his tense young body was on the alert, hands and mind ready to carry out his scheme. Once they struck an air-pocket that bounced Her Highness in a most undignified manner, rolling her over on her back as if she were a kitten, but she finally tumbled out of it, and spun on and on. Once the brother's eyes met and they grinned at each other reassuringly.

"Don't know what you're up to, Buddy, but I'm right with you," said Jim.

"Thanks. You might get your parachute in case I make a fluke. It's more likely to be that, than it is to do any good," answered Bob, for they could speak to each other quite easily now.

"How about your own umbrella?" Jim demanded.

"It's O. K.," answered Bob, then added, "See that road?"

"I can't help see it."

"Think there is room—I mean think it's wide enough so we can get into it without smashing the wings?"

"Ask me another. It's pretty narrow." Jim studied the situation. "That truck is wide and there's quite a space on each side, but it will take some fancy landing to get the wheels on the road and miss those trees at the side. They grow like a wall, and as they are coming up to meet us, they look like the bottom of a nice torture chamber bristling with sharpened spikes."

"Nothing wrong with the picture. Keep your eyes on that truck of Pedro's. I'm going to try to drop in front of it. They can't get by, or turn back, and all I hope to do is delay them, but that may help, if I do it. Keep a sharp lookout and tell me if I'm going too far either side. I don't want to get far ahead of them, not more than a few feet," Bob explained.

"Bully idea, old man. If we smash up, I'll meet you at the gate. If you need any help, I'll tell St. Peter you're a good kid and to let you in," Jim promised gravely.

"Go on. I'll have to do some tall lying to get him even to look at you," Bob retorted. "Here goes."

He started to manipulate the controls, slowly bringing Her Highness as he wanted her, and Jim scanned the scene ahead. He could see movement in the brush, men crawling or running on hands and knees, but not a uniform was in sight. He noted one thing in particular for which he was thankful. No one seemed to have noticed the falling plane, and that might be in their favor. Also, he thought ruefully, it might not. If the Mounties heard them dropping out of the sky, it would direct them more quickly to the road, but he thought of those men, armed to the teeth, desperate to get away, and he didn't try to imagine what they would do to the plane and the boys who threatened to frustrate their plans.

Austin had read of terrific battles with rum-runners who fought to the last ditch for their lives and stopped at nothing, and now he knew that if Her Highness was not hung in those spear-like pines, or wrecked on the treacherous road, the men behind them would instantly open fire and riddle them with bullets before they could move in the cock-pit. He glanced about for a sign of the Canadian officers, but not one did he see, and by now they were so close to the ground that his range of vision was very limited.

Then Bob brought Her Highness out of the spin, glided forward, her float ends scraping the edge of the truck as it slipped over, then, in another breathless second they were over the road, the wheels touched the ground, raced forward a few rods, slowed down, and at last came to a dead stop.

"Hey, what the blazes do you think you're doing?" It was the belligerent voice of the driver and did not sound at all like the musical tones of Pedro. Jim looked back while Bob loosened the safety strap, but did not get out of it.

"Hop over and tinker about," Bob directed, and Jim obeyed.

"You get out of the way," bellowed Pedro.

"Oh, hello, Old Man," Jim called good naturedly. "Our engine stalled. Guess we got something in it. Maybe you can give me a hand."

"I got no time. Get out of the way, fast. I'm in a hurry."

"Sorry, we won't be a minute." Bob was also struggling in the cock-pit as if something was out of order, and after a minute, during which Pedro made the air blue with curses, he got back in his seat.

"Guess we got it," he shouted. "Beastly sorry to keep you." Bob tried out the motor. It thundered smooth as silk, the plane moved a few inches, coughed apologetically, then stopped.

"Come on, now, old girl," Bob coaxed, and again he set the motor humming, but the propeller hung idle. Caldwell did not dare to move forward until he was ready to fly, for there wasn't a foot to spare on the road ahead, which curved sharply. Frantically the step-brothers tried out this and that, including the compass, but it didn't seem to help them a bit, and they were afraid to look over their shoulders at the fuming truck-man.

"What's the matter with her?" Pedro hadn't been able to sit still a moment longer, so he climbed from his seat and strode along the gully to the cock-pit.

"Hanged if I know. She never acted this way before," Jim answered innocently, and the man scowled savagely.

"What you doing here anyway?" Pedro persisted.

"Great guns," Bob looked up into the man's face. "Didn't you see us stall up there, and come down tail spinning! You are darned lucky we didn't smash up in front of you, that would have been something to cuss about. It takes hours to clear up a busted plane and she digs a hole in the ground ten feet deep. That would have held you up good and proper. Now, get back to your bus, we'll fix this thing as fast as we can and be out of your way."

"You kids look here." Pedro shook his fist in Bob's face. "You be out of here by the time I get my engine started, or I send you both to hell, fast, more fast than your plane," he promised.

"Thanks a lot, Old Timer. Every little favor is greatly appreciated," Bob answered, and he scowled quite as fiercely as the Canuck.

"And if you send us to hell this afternoon, maybe we won't be lonesome," Jim added. "Can you run a plane?"

"No," Pedro snapped savagely.

"Well, we can, but not if we're ghosts. Put that in your peace pipe and get on your own wave length. You don't own this end of Canada.

What are you doing here? If you can answer that, I've got another to ask you and it's right on the tip of my tongue—"

"Stick your tongue out at him," Bob suggested.

"I'd rather punch his jaw; I don't like his face. Give me that wrench and I'll tap him for sap, he's full of it. Run along, old boy—don't you know your onions, or haven't you got any this load?" Jim demanded.

"You get out of the way."

"You go back to your bus; you make us nervous so we can't tell whether the tail ensemble is in front or back—"

"You get out—" Pedro insisted, and then as the boys merely stared at him, he started toward the truck, and through a slit in the big car, Jim caught a glimpse of a man's face, and heard a soft signaling whistle as some one called the driver to his seat. Quickly the big fellow climbed up, and Jim, realizing that trouble was close by, buckled his safety strap, while Bob too made ready for a quick get-away.

"If I keep the engine going, it will locate us for those Mounties, but they're afoot, or horseback, and can't come so fast," Bob whispered.

"Start the noise and I'll watch behind. If I give you a kick in the ribs, lift us up," Jim replied under his breath. In a moment more the engine was racing again, then it really did stop, but this time it was by accident and looked as if it was too surprised to go, for at that instant, Bob caught sight of uniforms, and a sharp command was issued.

"Climb down out of that, Pedro." The boys looked back and saw the truck-driver's face turn green with terror. "Lively now, no funny business." Pedro literally tumbled to the ground, his legs shaking as if he had the ague, and his teeth chattering.

"I—I wasn't touching 'em," he stammered.

"Sure, I know you didn't, but you were impolite to American citizens and you ought to know better. Stand on your feet." Then the boys saw more than a dozen silent figures surrounding the truck.

"I didn't lay a hand on 'em," Pedro declared.

"It's well for you that you didn't send them to hell as you promised. What are you doing here and what have you got a green cover on your bus for? You went down the line this morning and you aren't reported back yet. Come, explain yourself." The man was on horseback and evidently the chief of the outfit. Jim guessed that he was playing for a few minutes to give his men time to close in, then he snapped again, "Cuff him. You boys let fly." Immediately the truck wagon was literally alive with men swarming over it. The doors at both ends were jerked open, and in another second, crouching outlaws were being tumbled over each other. Some of them opened fire, but their guns were knocked out of their hands, and in less time than it takes to tell about it, the fight was over. Fifteen prisoners were lined up on the road, while the officer looked at them calmly.

"Put them back in and take them along." The crowd was bundled back, this time each was securely handcuffed, then a familiar voice called from the woods.

"We got the last of them out of the hole, Chief. What shall we do with them?"

"Pile them in here," the Chief answered, then, as the group came stumbling forward, the man went on, but his voice was stern, "These your Texas friends, Bradshaw?"

"Yes sir," Bradshaw replied quickly.

"You'd better bring them to headquarters for obstructing traffic."

"All right, sir," Bradshaw agreed. "What'll we do with Her Highness? Put her under arrest?"

"Who is Her Highness?"

"The bus. I was introduced a few days ago."

"Thought United States didn't like nobility." There was a tiny smile on the chief's lips and a twinkle in his eyes. "How do you explain the title, Bradshaw?"

"I don't know, sir, unless they are of Irish descent—"

"We are not," Jim declared positively.

"You've done devilment enough today to be pure-bloods," Bradshaw informed them. The chief dismounted and came close to the fuselage and held out his hand.

"I want to thank you for your devilment, boys," he smiled and they both thought he was a grand looking man, the sort one reads about.

"We didn't do much of anything," Jim stammered.

"We like Canada," Bob added for he was less fussed and shook the officer's hand vigorously.

"If we've helped, we're mighty glad," Jim drawled, then went on, "But we'd have been wash-outs if it hadn't been for Her Highness. I think being among nobility made her do her job extra well."

"No doubt. Is she all right, or has something gone wrong with her?"

"Her Highness is fine as silk," Bob declared emphatically. "Nothing is the matter with her, Sir."

"Glad to hear it. Now, can you get her out of this trap?"

"Surely. It'll be a close shave, but she'll do it."

"All right. Wish you would and let the truck by. And, next time you are in Canada, look me up, there's something important I want to show you," the chief told them.

"We'll be mighty glad to see you—"

"But we're not coming if it's one of those parties with all the world looking on," Jim added quickly. The chief laughed.

"We'll spare your feelings, but if you'll come, we'd be glad to have you dine with us some evening, only just our own crowd—all these fellows you know, and the cook."

"That'll be fun," Jim agreed.

"We'll let you know some night when we're not having corned-beef and cabbage. So long."

"So long." Bob opened her up, the engine thundered, the propeller whirled madly. Her Highness slid forward, lifted, cleared the curve gracefully, zoomed and climbed. Both boys waved at the men, and a moment later Jim saw the truck load of outlaws being driven to some unknown point. That is, the point was not known to the boys, but they knew it was a good strong jail.

"It's been quite a day. Anything left in that basket?" Jim asked through the tube.

"Left in the basket! Well, if there is the squirrels are eating it back there in that ravine. You nut, you threw it overboard with your note," Bob answered.

"Great guns, so I did, and it's your Aunt's basket. Say, hop down in some town and let's buy another for her," Jim urged.

"Oh she won't mind, there's no hurry. We can get her one when we drive to North Hero," Bob objected.

"I know she won't mind, but just the same, let's get another to take back with us, and something because we lost the napkins and dishes," Jim insisted.

"Say, what's your rush?" Bob demanded impatiently.

"We want a basket again, don't we? Don't we want to go up tomorrow? Well, we can't lose all your aunt's baskets and expect her to pack grub stakes for us, can we?" Jim answered.

"That's so. We better get her a couple," Bob agreed quickly. He consulted the map. "St. John's is the nearest," he announced, so gravely he turned Her Highness' nose in the direction of the town, because, when the matter was put to him that way, he could see the need of keeping Mrs. Fenton supplied with baskets.

VIII
ABLAZE

For the next three days after the boys' exploit in Canada, it rained. Not gentle showers, but a good stiff down-pour that drenched the land, swelled the Lake, and ruined young crops. Her Highness was kept in the carriage shed under the tool house, because besides raining as if it were never going to stop, there was thunder and lightning, and hours of pitch blackness. Both Jim and Bob would have liked nothing better than to go soaring up and battle with the elements but they knew that such an adventure would cause Mrs. Fenton terrific worry every moment they were out of her sight, so they contented themselves with the radio, phonograph, some jolly old books they found in the attic, and swims between storms. Several times they caught glimpses of the strange boy as he went splashing by to and from the garden, and they watched his run-off with considerable interest.

"If he keeps the water down on that hole land it will save the alfalfa meadow," Mr. Fenton remarked thoughtfully.

"Does he seem to be doing it, Uncle Norman?"

"So far the water isn't any higher."

"Jinks, that's great," Jim exclaimed with enthusiasm. He rather envied Corso's young nephew who disregarded weather and waded barefoot along the road, his overalls rolled above his knees, and not even a splattering automobile racing past him, sending sheets of water from all four wheels, seemed to disturb him.

The morning of the fourth day broke clear and fine, the sky velvet blue, and not a cloud in sight. The step-brothers came down stairs with joyous whoops, and young Caldwell danced his aunt about the kitchen.

"Well, my land, if you want me to dance with you Bob, you will have to make it a reel or a jig—"

"Let it be a jig," Bob answered promptly and taking her hand he began the clattery dance while Jim played an accompaniment on the mouth organ. But in a few minutes Mrs. Fenton had to stop for breath.

"Where did you learn to do that?" she demanded. "I never supposed that any young one could do it these days."

"In school," Bob answered. "You ought to see Jim Highland Fling."

"What's all the shouting about?" Mr. Fenton asked. He had just come in with the brimming milk pails.

"Look at the weather," Jim laughed.

"It's enough to make an airplane do a tail spin," Bob added.

"No doubt, but I hope Her Highness doesn't do any more—"

"More?" The boys chorused.

"Canadian chap telephoned me yesterday to inquire if you live here, and he said that you two had made the country safe for the Mounted Police—"

"Aw, go on," Bob exclaimed in disgust.

"What did they do that for?" demanded Jim.

"In the course of his duty," Mr. Fenton smiled. "We'll be very much obliged if you will give us the details of the war while we breakfast. We want to know all about it. It isn't every day that exciting things happen around us and we feel that we have been slighted—"

"That's all right, Mr. Fenton. Bob did most of it. I'll tell you the whole story—"

"I did not do most of it," Bob denied emphatically. "If you leave out anything you did, I'll tell them."

"Fair enough," Mr. Fenton laughed. "Now sit down, satisfy the first pangs of hunger, then begin," he ordered, and the boys took their places.

Between the two of them, the Fentons were able to get a fairly interesting account of what happened, and when the story was finished, Mrs. Fenton looked at them soberly.

"My, my, you might both have been killed. That was why you got me those new baskets. I thought there was something queer about your losing it," Mrs. Fenton exclaimed. "If you had lost it, or forgotten it, I should not have minded one bit; but if you had told me how you happened to throw it overboard, I should have been glad."

"We wanted to be sure that we had a basket for next time," Bob grinned cheerfully. "We expect there will be other next times."

"My land of goodness, there's the mail man. He looks like a drowned rat. Come right in, Harvey." The R.F.D. man wore boots that came to his thigh, and even at that he was splashed with mud.

"Got a registered letter, and another one that looks important, so I didn't put them in the box," the man explained. "Some rain we've had. Did you know, Fenton, that the Carrying Point is covered? The water is going over it like a mill race, and I had all I could do to keep the wheels under me. Loaded the car up with rocks or I'd have been swimming around after the letters."

"My land sakes alive, is it as bad as that! Here Jim, this letter seems to be for you." Mrs. Fenton gave Austin a long envelope, which he accepted with surprise. In the corner was a Canadian stamp.

"Looks like it's from your friends across the border," Mr. Fenton said. Jim opened it promptly, and scanned the contents, then he smiled with relief that it wasn't more formidable. The salutation was as he had signed the note he dropped to the Mounties in the Ravine.

'Flying Buddies.

Gentlemen:

It would give us great pleasure if you will join us in an informal dinner tomorrow evening at seven P.M. In going over the off duty hours, we find that most of the men who participated in the affair at the ravine can be present. You have our solemn word that the dinner is merely a friendly one, and you will not be embarrassed by speeches. As a matter of fact you may be aroused to the fighting point by the uncomplimentary remarks of your hosts. Telephone me if the time is not convenient to you, and believe me,

Very sincerely yours,

Allen Ruhel.'

"Great guns and little fish-hooks, that will be fun," Bob shouted.

"It means tonight," Jim reminded his step-brother.

"It says tomorrow."

"But it's dated yesterday."

"That's so. We'll get Her Highness diked out, and be ready. Suppose we better wear real clothes under our flying suits—"

"Dinner coats," Jim agreed. "If it's informal we don't have to do more than that—"

"Brush our teeth," Bob suggested. They showed the letter to the Fentons and the man looked grave.

"I hope they are careful what they say," he remarked seriously.

"What do you mean?" Bob demanded.

"These international affairs are ticklish things. If you get riled and throw a soup plate, or some little thing like that, it might bring on a war. It doesn't take much to bring on a war—"

"There isn't a soup plate handy, Uncle Norman, but I know where Aunt Belle keeps her potato masher. You want to be very careful that you do not start any internal wars; they are the worst sort."

"Guess I better get outside if that's the case," he chuckled, and went for his own high boots.

"Let's have a look at the world," Jim proposed, then added, "Old Champlain looks kind of high to me. Is it usually so?"

"Suppose it would be after so much rain," Bob put in.

"No it isn't," Mrs. Fenton answered, and she looked very serious. "It's higher now than it's been in years, and with the rain stopped, it will fill more. There are so many streams, some big ones, that empty into it all around." She went with the boys to the back veranda and glanced across anxiously. "I can't see Gull Rock at all, and Fisher's Island looks as if half of it is under water."

"If it comes flooding too high, we'll take you and Uncle Norman up in Her Highness out of danger," Bob promised.

"We can get in the boats if necessary, Bob, and we've got a lot of high land for the stock, so that will be all right, but there are many of the people here who have small farms. My land sakes alive, I expect that some of them are in a bad way right this minute. I'll go telephone." She hurried into the house, and in a moment the boys heard her talking with some neighbors.

"Let's have a walk around," Bob suggested.

"We won't need to wheel Her Highness out. Look at the carriage shed," Jim exclaimed as he happened to glance in that direction and saw the water lapping up under the wide doors.

"Cracky. Let's see if she's all right."

"We'll have to take our shoes off—or get boots."

"I'll see if Aunt Belle has any extra pairs around." He went inside, while Jim surveyed the turbulent waters which had risen several feet and were thrashing up to the edge of Mrs. Fenton's flower garden, and was more than half way across the lawn when the two boys first saw it.

"Come on," Bob called, and Jim went inside to the shed. "Here are some boots. Aunt Belle says they are water-proof, but not very handsome. They have been patched."

"They will be just the thing." Presently the pair had their feet in boots several sizes too large for them, but they grinned, and went down into the yard. Their first care was Her Highness. The water had run up a little way under her, but she hadn't suffered any damage. Jim got into the cock-pit and shifted the wheels to the floats, and that done the boys continued the tour of inspection.

"If it rains any more, by George, there will be the deuce to pay." They went to the edge of the Lake, but could not follow its rim because the inundations were deep and many of them ended in treacherous swampy stretches. Where the cedar-rimmed cliff came close to the lake's edge, the water pounded high above all previous marks, and some of the lower ones were being undermined by the strength of the waves.

"Looks like a regular ocean," Jim remarked thoughtfully as they stood on a promontory which jutted out in defiance of Old Champlain's fury. "Say, where's that Carrying Point?"

"Further down. About half way to the village. Remember the day we were coming up and you noticed a neck of land, lake on both sides, that connected the two larger sections of North Hero?"

"Oh sure. Little stretch with a beach and roadway."

"That's it. Mom told me it got its name from Revolutionary days. Pirates and smugglers coming down from Canada with loads of goods in small boats, carried their boats across this piece and would get away from the officers, or whoever happened to be chasing them. It's quite historic. A bigger craft coming along would have to go all the way around and by that time the smugglers could lose them plenty. They'd hide among some of the lower islands, or even go on straight."

"Great old place. Obliging of Champlain to arrange itself so conveniently. Smashing guns, look at that water. It's hammering in all directions. Too bad if it spoils crops, but it sure looks as if it is going to. Did you hear your Aunt say whether the turkeys are dying off because of the dampness?"

"Hezzy reported a hundred have turned up their toes."

"Rotten. Why don't they have a good warm place to keep them when the weather is had?" Jim exclaimed wrathfully.

"That's the funny part of it, Buddy, they have got a real up-to-the-minute house, brooders and everything," Bob replied soberly, then added, "Gosh, I do wish we could do something about it."

"Well, we can't keep them from dying off, that's a cinch," Jim answered. "Let's take Her Highness and have a look over the place."

"Right-O, old man." They turned about away from the destructive waters and hurried as fast as the clumsy boots would permit, to the carriage house, where they floated the plane out, closed the door after them, and piled into the cock-pit. "Got enough gas?"

"Plenty."

Presently Her Highness was thundering above the lake and after a few circles over the land, which gave the boys an idea of the havoc being wrought among the islands, Jim headed her toward the end of Isle La Motte and in a few minutes they were cruising at low speed above the turkey farm. It too had suffered from the rain, but its buildings were located on high ground which was well drained so that even now it was drying rapidly. The boys could see the turkeys in the run-ways and they knew that until the vicinity was no longer drenched, the delicate birds could not be allowed to roam in the larger pens. As there seemed to be nothing special they could learn, they proceeded to fly across the property, and soon they were above the section where they had seen the men hiking the first day they had attempted to visit Hezzy. Just beyond the strip of forest, which was quite dense, they saw a long, comparatively bare slope toward the opposite side of the Isle and they easily discerned several men moving about as if they were working.

"There's more turkeys," Jim remarked through the tube and Bob nodded that he could see them.

"Probably they are fixing a place on this side because it's more sheltered," the younger boy suggested. "I see Hezzy down there." Sure enough the farm's foreman was striding along the edge of the meadow. He paused suddenly, glanced up at them, then disappeared quickly among the trees.

"I suspect that he doesn't like us," Jim grinned, and Bob laughed heartily.

"Sometime we'll come over and tell him we want to help catch the thieves," the younger boy suggested.

"Let's hop down now. We can land on that field."

"We'd better not. We might land on some small birds," Bob replied, and Jim agreed that probably it would be safer to wait and have their talk with Hezzy at the house. As there didn't seem to be much more to see the boys rode on, across to the New York side of Champlain, and before they decided to return they were overtaken by the mail plane.

Bob, who was at the controls, waggled his wings, and instantly the other pilot responded. He grinned as he flew by, and they waved as if he were an old friend.

"It's the guy we saw the other day," Jim declared, and Bob nodded.

The mail plane went racing north, and the boys started for home. It felt good being in the air again, but they were going to the dinner and they wanted to give Her Highness her weekly inspection, besides replenish the gas supply. That evening, with their best suits under flying togs, they hopped off again, this time making straight north toward the border. They soared grandly beneath a brilliant dome of colors reflected by the setting sun, roared above Canada, and in half an hour came down on the flying field where they found Allen Ruhel and Sergeant Bradshaw, their uniforms swank, and their faces wearing wide grins of welcome.

"Glad you could come," Ruhel greeted them.

"We surely owe you a swell spread—" Bradshaw began, but the chief interrupted him.

"Perhaps we do, but they are not going to get much more than the usual mess. I had to promise that or they would not have come."

"How's Pat?" Bob inquired as they were led toward the long mess hall.

"He's so set up over my promotion there's no doing anything with him," Bradshaw answered soberly. "I may have to trade him off for a yellow cat."

"Any time you want to trade him, let us know," Jim put in quickly.

"I know you boys. You'd spoil him more than I have."

They were ushered into a barracks-like building and were soon in the mess hall where already two dozen of Canada's finest men were waiting. The boys recognized a few of their faces, though not many, but introductions were gotten over with little ceremony, and the dinner started. Because of the young American guests of honor there was no wine served, but that did not detract from anyone's good humor, and the party was an enormous success. Bradshaw told the boys that the outlaw gang they had been trying to capture for such a long time, were at last almost all rounded up.

"Thanks to your good help," he added. "Jinks, wish we could have been down in the battle," Bob lamented.

"I say, didn't you have enough of it?" the chief laughed. "It seems to me you were rather in the thick of things, you know. I expected any moment the blighters would turn their guns on your wings. They would have made their get-away if you had not let us know about the hole they were crawling through. Did Bradshaw tell you that it was fitted up like a war-time trench, with living quarters, periscopes and what-not?"

"Great guns—oh, what happened to Pedro?"

"He's a perfectly good Canuck gone wrong. He'll pay for his sins with the rest. A couple of them got away, and a few of the ones we caught are Americans."

"Do you have to send them back?" Jim asked. He rather felt the fellows should take their punishment with their gang.

"Neither your government nor their families have shown any disposition to intervene in their behalf," the chief smiled, then went on, "As a matter of fact, from their records in the States, I think your Department of Justice is likely to send us a vote of thanks for apprehending them."

"I hope they do," Jim responded. After that the courses went on merrily. There were jokes, jolly stories, no end of kidding back and forth, and finally the dessert was served. A few minutes later the chief rose.

"I promised our American friends that there would be no speeches tonight, so I've kept my word, but some of the boys will have a presentation. Stand up, you men of Texas, and take your medicine."

The boys obeyed, and flushed crimson around their collars as the chief made his way to their places. He opened a small box which seemed to have some ribbons on the royal purple velvet surface. The man held them up and solemnly pinned one to each boy's coat. Each medal was of two ribbons, the American flag and the British, arranged on a bar side by side, and suspended from them was the Mounty Insignia in the middle, a pair of wings, and from the wings hung a tiny basket.

"To the Flying Buddies"

was engraved on the back.

"You can thank your lucky stars that this isn't the French section of Canada and you don't have to be kissed," Bradshaw informed them.

"We're grateful for that," Jim laughed in confusion.

"This has been a swell party, but what we did, if it was any good, was as much for our own country as for yours, but let me tell you this, if we ever catch you in Texas, we'll get back at you—we'll pin horseshoes on every one of you," Bob declared.

"Is that a threat or a promise?"

"Both," Bob laughed.

"My Dad has a sizy sort of ranch. It will hold the whole bunch, so if any of you come to our state we'll be mortally offended if you don't show up at our house," Jim supplemented. He was recovering his poise, and then the Mounties cheered them until the rafters rang. An hour later they were allowed to depart, and every man promised to call for the horseshoe.

"That was a dandy party," Jim chuckled later as they circled above the field again.

"They are a grand bunch," Bob declared enthusiastically. He leveled off Her Highness, and started in a southerly course that would take them down over New York state a way, but the wind was from the west and would drive them toward their own goal. The night was starless, although there seemed to be few clouds, and the air was heavy with moisture as if it would be raining before morning. The step-brothers did no more talking. They were both busy with their own thoughts. Their minds were occupied with the evening's fun, but in a few minutes Bob began to think of his aunt and uncle and wished very hard that he could do something to help them. The rain had ruined a large part of the crops, and although there was time to plant other things, the year promised to be another bad one for the Fentons. The boy resolved to write and tell his mother. Mom somehow always had a suggestion that was worth while. If we could only find out what happens to the turkeys, he sighed and he resolved to pay Hezzy a visit the next day if possible. Suddenly, in the distance they caught a glimpse of a flash of light across the sky. It disappeared almost at once, then they picked it up again.

"Bet it's the mail plane," Jim shouted.

"Guess it is," Bob agreed. He watched the plane getting closer, and presently there was no mistaking the huge machine that came droning toward them. Their altitude was five thousand feet, and the other pilot would pass almost over them. It was mighty chummy to meet a pal of the air, so Bob zoomed up, and soon Her Highness was racing beside the bigger machine. The pilots waved greetings, waggled their wings, then, as the boys had to turn eastward, they waved a good-night, turned abruptly and shot across the other's course. The man in the cock-pit nodded, and in a minute they were a mile apart, but Jim was watching the diminishing lights with interest. Suddenly he caught his brother's arm and twisted him around.

"Something's gone wrong," he bellowed; He didn't need to, for Bob could see. At that moment there was a blaze, a leaping tongue of flame and the plane started to totter crazily toward the ground.

"Thundering Mars—he's on fire!"

IX
THE MAIL MUST GO THROUGH

"Bellowing Bulls," Bob yelled at the top of his lungs as he realized that something catastrophic was taking place in the air and that the good-natured young pilot was in danger of his life.

"Blistering blazes," Jim exclaimed. Neither boy could hear the other's ejaculation, but they were tense and rigid as they sat for a paralyzed instant staring through the darkness toward that flaming plane which was beginning to drop like some kind of lost star out of the blackness of the sky.

Mechanically young Caldwell kicked the rudder, his fingers adjusted the controls, and Her Highness came around with a screech of the wind through the struts and a shrill whine of the wires. He opened her up wide, zoomed, then leveling off, raced toward that flaming, careening plane. With lightning rapidity the boy calculated to a nicety the speed of the doomed mail-plane, and into both their brains flashed the ghastly question as to the sort of spot on to which she was making her plunge. Was it smooth open country, or was it thick forests where the fire would spread and become a violent furnace before it could be subdued, or was it into some little sleeping village, whose residents would be seriously jeopardized?

As she made her way downward the plane cast a bright glow about herself, like a funeral bier, but the light only accentuated the night beyond the rim. At racing speed Her Highness cut through the heavens like a thin streak of brightness, and in a minute she was above her falling fellow. The altimeter read three thousand feet, so Bob climbed higher, circled when he was sure he would have the grade he wanted, then, tipping the nose almost vertical, he raced downward, the engine roaring. It was breath-taking, but both boys were keenly alert. In a moment they were beside the burning plane and following it, at a safe distance, toward the ground.

They could see the mail pilot struggling with the controls, then he noticed them, grinned, and with a wave of his hand, he stopped the battle, loosened his safety strap, and stepped over the rim of the cock-pit. He seemed as cool as if he were doing a stunt at a fair-ground. A moment later he waved again, then jumped into space, making as wide a leap as possible. The two machines plunged on and the man's body seemed to roll, then drop swiftly, then the parachute blossomed out wide and white as it spread open to save him.

"Whew," Bob whistled softly. He could not watch the escaping pilot a moment longer, but he switched on all the light he had in an effort to pick out a landing place. One thing they were positive of, they were not over a village, for there wasn't even a fueling signal visible. On they went, and at last Jim caught his step-brother's shoulder.

"Woods," he said, making his lips form the word so the boy would get it, and Bob nodded that he understood. By this time they were so close to the ground that the descending furnace cast a brighter glow, and they could see the tree tops standing out like sentinels. At five hundred feet Bob pulled Her Highness out of the mad drop, leveled off and circled in swift short turns. He maintained the height, and the two looked over the side. Presently they saw the pilot dropping toward them for his speed had been checked by the parachute. At the same instant there was a dull thud and the mail plane smashed into the ground. The flames leaped furiously, and while they ate hungrily at their prey, they lighted the vicinity brilliantly.

"Over there," Jim pointed, and Bob looked. He saw a clear place, and shutting off the motor, glided to a landing. Before Her Highness came to a full stop, Jim was out of the cock-pit. He glanced anxiously at the work of destruction, then looked up to the pilot, but he gasped with dismay as he discovered that the fellow was over trees and seemed unable to spill enough air to guide himself out of their reach. In a second a huge branch caught the silk and held it firmly, while the man dangled like a pendulum thirty feet above the hard ground. A fall would mean broken bones.

As the step-brothers were Texans first and foremost, ranchers' sons, they never went anywhere without a rope. In fact they would have felt as if they were not fully dressed, so now long lariats were coiled under their seats. It took only a second to secure them, then the two raced toward the tree.

"Hey you lads, get the mail out of the plane," the pilot shouted when he saw them approaching.

"You go back and do that while I get him down," Jim said quickly to his brother. "The three of us can probably save it all."

"Take my rope." Bob handed it over, then started to save the mail or as much of it as he could, while Austin ran on to the tree.

"Be careful. I'm trying to figure out a way to get onto the branch, but if I swing. I'll come down," the pilot called.

"I'll look out. Hold yourself steady." Jim had the rope in his hands, but a flying suit is a cumbersome garment and hampering. He stood away on a slight knoll, gave the lariat a few expert turns, then sent it forth. It shot under the pilot's feet, opened wide, rose quickly and was jerked securely.

"Good work, Buddy," the pilot called.

"Fix it so it won't cut you and I'll get in that nearest tree," Jim answered. He was already beside the tree, and looping the end of the rope about his wrist as he started to climb. It was no easy task to prevent the lariat from tangling with the branches, but luckily the tree was a yellow pine, and one side of its trunk had only a few short stubs. The boy went like a monkey and was soon a few feet higher than the pilot. He fastened the end of the rope to a stout branch, took an instant to decide what his next move would be, then he made up his mind, and began to crawl out closer to the man he was trying to save.

"Careful that doesn't smash," the chap warned.

"All right. Get loose from your parachute. I'll make a hitch here, so you'll come just under me—"

"Sure that will hold us both?"

"It's a good green branch."

"You make your hitch, then get back to the trunk," the pilot proposed. "It will be safer." Jim obeyed. Hanging on with one hand, he leaned forward to watch. The pilot released himself from the straps, then eased himself by hanging on with one hand. Finally he let go, and swung beneath by the lariat. Vigorously he sent his body forward, grasped the branch, hauled himself upright, then made his way to his rescuer.

"All O. K."

"I'll tell the world. Come along and we'll help the kid." Scrambling to the ground was much simpler than making the ascent, and presently they joined young Bob, who was courageously hauling out bags of mail.

"Gosh," he whistled.

"Here, take hold." The pilot directed the work and in a few minutes the mail bags were all out of the compartment, and none too soon, for the flames had gained great headway, and were swiftly devouring the plane. They dragged the bags to a safe distance.

"I say, we have some Pyrene," Bob announced; "I was a boob not to think of it before." He ran for the tank, they helped him with the tiny hose, and in a few minutes the blaze was extinguished. The darkness seemed to settle about them more thickly than ever, but the light from Her Highness showed clearly so they could see their way to the plane. Quickly the mail pilot glanced over it and he smiled with admiration.

"Some grand little bus," he told them.

"You bet. Where can we take you?"

"To Albany. We got to get the mail there too," the pilot informed them and the brothers glanced at each other. Her Highness would certainly carry the three of them and some freight, but whether she was capable of such a load was another matter. "The mail must get through," the pilot repeated. "We'll try it," Jim responded.

"One of you fellows might stay here," the pilot suggested.

"That won't be necessary," Jim said quickly. Taking the mail to Albany would be a task, but coming back to find the one left behind would be an all night's job. Anyway, Her Highness had never been pressed into service for such an emergency and he was determined to leave nothing behind if that could be avoided. The mail man was already dragging bags from the pile. Luckily none of them were very bulky and the three set to work to fit them into the freight compartment. That full, what was left was stored in the extra passenger seat.

"I'll sit back there," Bob offered. "I'm smallest."

"All right," Jim agreed. He was rather glad the younger boy had made the suggestion. Caldwell had piloted Her Highness through her latest hazard and must be fagged. "Pile in." He took a moment to inspect the strip he would follow in the take-off, then leaped to his own seat. The third air-man was beside him.

"I'm much obliged to you lads for what you did for me tonight," he said. "You don't know what a relief it was to see you tearing to help me. Had an idea that your backs were turned in my direction and didn't hope that you had seen me."

"I was watching you as we went along. We were about a mile over, so of course we came back," Jim replied casually. "Glad we were able to get to you in time."

Further conversation was impossible, for the boy opened the throttle and Her Highness roared. The engine ran smoothly, the machine started, but it seemed to Jim as if she would never lift. He could see the pines leaping toward them, then up went her nose and she was off the ground, soared laboriously and dangerously close to the trees, then began to climb. That part accomplished, Austin was relieved, and he concentrated on the long grill ahead of him. He wished that he had discussed the course with this man who must know every inch of air along his route, but the whole affair had taken but a short time. The excitement had driven a great many things from his mind, so now he began to calculate his course, tracing it on the map. In coming up from Texas the boys had stopped off to see the capital city and its twin across the river. He could depend upon the pilot to direct him to the proper field, so coming down would be all right.

The unaccustomed load made Her Highness' management quite different from ordinary occasions when she had carried only an extra passenger, but the mail had to go through, regardless of men and machines, and the youthful part-owner of the plane was proud of her performance now, but he hoped hard that they would meet nothing on the way which would add to their difficulties. He thought of the Fentons. They were early birds and probably in bed long ago, but Bob's aunt was a nervous woman and she might not sleep soundly because of their absence. They could let her know from Albany what was delaying them, but that might only add to her anxiety. Well, they had to make the best of it and it was rather an honor to be entrusted with U. S. mail. He tried to imagine what the bags contained. Probably a great many of the letters were highly important. People would not be sending their communications by the swiftest way if the matters were not urgent.

On, on, and on they soared through the night. The clock on the dial said twelve thirty. It seemed much longer than that since they had left their jolly hosts in Canada. Once the mail pilot touched his arm, then raising his hand as if he were an orchestra leader, he motioned to go higher, Jim nodded that he understood, so began to climb. They were fifteen thousand feet when he got the signal to level off. Then he pointed to the speaking tube, and the pilot nodded that he would use it if he had anything to say. One o'clock came, and one-thirty. They had been going over an hour. Probably the mail was late, for Jim was sure the regular plane was a fast bus. Her Highness could do high speed too, but not with such a load. It was nearly two o'clock when the pilot picked up the tube and gave directions. Later he pointed.

"There's the field." It was brilliantly lighted and the boy could see figures moving about the drome. As he glided down he noticed men looking at him curiously. He decided that they expected the mail plane and were surprised at his arrival. When he came to a stop a chap ran to the fuselage.

"Seen anything of Mason—the—"

"Right here, Old Timer," Mason said quickly.

"Thank the Lord. We got word that a blazing plane was sighted, and we've been on pins and needles ever since. A couple of Canadians are out trying to locate you."

"I'm O. K., and so is the mail, thanks to these youngsters." Mason prepared to hop out, and he turned to Jim. "You didn't tell me your name. I'm Phil Mason."

"Mine's Jim Austin, and my step-brother is Bob Caldwell. We've been visiting relatives in Vermont," Jim explained. By that time Bob was out of his seat and a couple of men were removing the bags.

"Glad to know you lads. You want to bunk here the rest of the night—"

"Thanks, no, but I should appreciate a supply of gas. I'm not sure I have enough to make the trip back," Jim answered.

"Gas, of course, you can have all you want. Here you—" He shouted directions, and a mechanic came on the run. The task of re-fueling was accomplished with efficiency, but the boys had to shake hands with a lot of relieved pilots who were grateful that one of their number was not lying wrecked and helpless miles away. Finally they permitted the buddies to go, and this time Bob was beside his brother.

"Want me to pilot, old man?" he offered.

"Did you get any sleep back there?" Jim demanded.

"No, I watched the duplicate controls. Thought you might need help."

"Then you sit beside me and take a nap now. If I get so my eyes won't stay open. I'll wake you up and let you do the work," Jim promised.

"So long, Buddies," Mason shouted, just as the throttle was opened. Bob waved his hand, and Jim nodded. Taking off on the drome was simple, and in a moment Her Highness, no longer loaded to the hilt, leaped into the air.

"Great old girl," Jim exclaimed proudly, and the plane responded eagerly. The course was set, and while they went, roaring back toward the northern part of Vermont, Bob's head nodded and finally dropped forward as sleep overtook him. Jim grinned affectionately at the young fellow and made up his mind that he wouldn't disturb that rest if he could possibly help it.

The trip home was uneventful but Jim did have to blink hard several times to keep his eyes open. However, he managed it, but the first streaks of dawn were softening the sky before the Fenton Cove met his tired vision. With a whistle of relief that at last it was over, he glided down toward the carriage house, and as the plane shot forward, he heard the house door open quickly.

"Is that you, boys?" Mrs. Fenton's tone was distressed. Then Bob woke up, blinked, and stared.

"Thunder and Mars, why didn't you let me do part of it?" he demanded.

"We're all right," Jim shouted to Aunt Belle, and added to his step-brother, "I'll let you have the honor of putting her ladyship up if you like."

"You'd better," Bob growled. "Next time I won't go to sleep. You go in and hop to bed. I'll explain to Aunt Belle." That arrangement was entirely satisfactory to Jim, and in five minutes he was in their room, in ten minutes he was stretched out in his pajamas and sound asleep. It was noon when he opened his eyes. Bob was on the second cot and was just turning over.

"Hello, Old Timer."

"Hello yourself. What day is it?"

"Same one. Say, Jim did you notice the lake when we got home?"

"Didn't notice a blooming thing. Is the house afloat?"

"Not yet. It rained some more. Woke me up about nine o'clock. I'd thought of going over today and have a talk with Hezzy, but I changed my mind," Bob announced.

"Wise lad."

"You never did cotton up to Hezzy did you?"

"Not so you could notice it."

"Well, I've been doing some thinking. Seems kind of queer to me that he should have sneaked under those trees yesterday when we were going over. I've been wondering what he was doing on that side of the property. If it was all right, what the heck did he dodge us for?"

"Ask me another," Jim yawned. "Did your Aunt think we had flown to the bottom of the lake?"

"She sure did, but luckily she didn't miss us until she got up. Our door was open and she saw the beds—then she got scared for fair and came flying down stairs. About that time we came rolling in. I am glad she didn't have any more time to fret."

"Same here." Just then they heard Mrs. Fenton come tip-toeing up the stairs and they both closed their eyes tight, then began to snore melodiously. Anyone could tell that it was a pretense.

"I was just coming to see if you boys aren't ready to have something to eat. You must be starved," she exclaimed.

"We are," they wailed.

"Well, dinner's all ready. You get into your bath-robes and come right down. No one will mind and I guess you deserve some privileges. Someone called up this morning to know if you got home all right, and I guess you did more than Bob told me." She looked reproachfully at her nephew and shook her finger. "Now, hustle up—I've got huckleberry pie—" They were out of bed before the words were fairly uttered, so she hurried back to her duties and the two boys were close at her heels, donning bath robes as they came. They did take time to have a good cold splash, and glance at the lake, which had risen two feet higher.

Mr. and Mrs. Fenton tried to look cheerful and to joke during the meal, but it was not a success, for the menacing water creeping steadily toward them had already seeped into the cellar, and on the road in front of the house the boys could see automobiles, trucks, hay wagons, and even a team of oxen hitched to a great cart, plugging slowly forward. The vehicles were every one of them piled high with household effects and the people of the island whose homes were already below the danger line, were looking for a safe place to settle until Champlain should recede within bounds. The meal over, the two boys went to the veranda at the back. There was something terrible about the whole situation, and they wondered dully what could be done about it. Just waiting was nerve racking. For a minute they watched the water, which was muddy as it thrashed in the rising wind, and beyond the cove they could see branches, whole trees, rails of fences, boxes, and all sorts of wreckage tossed on the waves.

"Let's get out of sight of it," Bob proposed, so they went to the front of the house, but the view there was no less depressing. An old man trudged through the water driving his cow, and right behind him, seated on a queer old carriage was his wife driving a horse that lifted his hoofs wearily and wheezed with every step. At that moment an automobile drove to the door, and a huge man, with a booming voice, stuck his head out of the window.

"Can I get something to eat here?"

"Come right in," Mrs. Fenton answered. The man climbed out clumsily, and right behind him came a smaller man who had been completely concealed by his companion.

"This is a blasted neck of the woods," the big fellow bellowed.

"Let's sit over here," Bob suggested. He didn't think the newcomer added anything attractive to the prevailing discomfort. The fellow talked and cussed the weather, but the small man didn't utter a word. It wasn't until they were eating that he ventured to speak.

"I told you, Burnam, this was a fool's errand," he declared. The big man brought his fist down on the table so hard that the china jumped.

"Don't I know you did. Well, I'm telling you that they are hiding somewhere around here, understand, and I'm going to find them. You can get on the train and go to blazes if you like, see!" The words and the tone made the boys jump, then Jim gripped Bob's arm.

"Shhhhsss." He pointed to the end of the veranda. Bob looked and was surprised to see Corso standing like a statue close to the step. He looked as if something had struck him paralyzed, but he recovered himself in a second, leaped nimbly to the veranda, stepped with amazing swiftness to the window and cautiously peeped in. It was just one brief glance he got of the room and the tourists, but it seemed to be enough. He jumped lightly as a cat to the ground, crouched, then disappeared around the corner of the house.

"What do you know about that," Bob exclaimed, then added quickly, "Don't tell me to ask you another. Let's go up and get our clothes on."

X
DANGER!!

"I say, Jim, that was a queer thing for Corso to do!" The two were putting the finishing touches on their toilet. From the dining room came the voice of the man called Burnam, who seemed to do considerable talking while he ate, but if his companion spoke again, his words were inaudible.

"Yes. Listen, Buddy, I think Corso knows that lad down there."

"Maybe he does," Bob agreed, but that hadn't occurred to him.

"Maybe we can help those two. Come on down, and if the bounders show a disposition to pump us, let's give them an earful."

"Great guns, we don't want to tell him they are here—"

"Of course not, you nut. We'll see what they lead up to. You follow my lead. Come along." They raced down stairs quietly and into the dining room. Mrs. Fenton had finished serving the travelers and had gone to the cellar where she was rescuing preserves.

"Good car you have," Jim remarked, and Burnam glanced at him.

"Pretty good," he admitted. "Know anything about cars?"

"Enough to run a flivver," Jim answered modestly. Burnam sized them up as a pair of country hicks and smiled broadly.

"Interesting neighborhood around here," he ventured.

"Oh, fair," Jim drawled.

"Not many strangers," Burnam went on.

"A sprinklin', but nobody wants them," Jim volunteered.

"Exclusive community. What do you do with strangers?"

"Leave 'em alone. There's a colony further up. Summer people, most from cities, come every year."

"Same ones all the time?"

"Sure. Fellow who owns the land won't let 'em bring outsiders," the boy explained taking a chair. "Enjoy your dinner?"

"Fine. Ever have any southern people—"

"Few," Jim admitted.

"Chap I know and his nephew came around here for the fishing. He liked the place. Perhaps you know him."

"How long has he been coming?" Jim asked.

"I understand last fall was the first time, come to think of it."

"Nobody was here last fall," Jim declared positively. "What sort of chap is he, about your size?"

"No, very slender fellow, dark skin and eyes, rather good looking." Jim looked at Bob.

"Maybe it's those ginks," he said scornfully.

"Sounds like them," Bob admitted.

"Where they stopping?" Burnam asked, eagerly.

"They ain't," Jim grinned, then added, "They tried this neighborhood for a week, then went on into Canada. The station agent said their luggage was shipped to Toronto."

"You don't say." The big man seemed disappointed and the little one smiled behind his napkin.

"Chap like that wouldn't stay in so small a place," he remarked.

"No, I suppose not. Well, can I pay you—"

"Pay my brother," Jim answered, and strolled out of the house. In the soft earth he had no difficulty in trailing Corso's foot prints and a few minutes later saw the man and the boy crouched in the garden where they were completely hidden from the road. "Hello," he said softly. "I told those fellows that you two went to Toronto. Know where that is?"

"I do," Corso answered.

"I let them ask me questions, then told them you stayed here a week. They are so disgusted with the place I don't think they'll hang around, but you better keep out of sight. I'm going to escort them off the island, but they don't know that."

"Much in your debt we are, Sir," Corso said quietly. "We shall not forget, Sir." His eyes turned toward the road. "Bad men, Sir. Very, very bad men."

"They don't look any too good," Jim admitted. "You stay here until one of us comes and tells you they are gone." Jim strode quickly back toward the house and as he crossed the road he saw Burnam getting into the limousine.

"Get a move on, Dyke," he growled, and the smaller chap hastily took his place. Motioning to his step-brother to keep quiet, Jim stepped behind the huge maple, and when the car hacked into the road, he hopped onto the spare tires, caught the strap and threw his legs over, ducking his head so that if the men should either of them glance through the window, he would not be seem. The car raced off carrying the stow-a-way. "I told you those lads were in this part of the country," Burnam said shrilly when they had gone some distance from Stumble Inn. "I know just how to handle natives, and I got exactly the information we want."

"Yes, but how the blazes do you expect to pick up the trail in Canada?" Dyke demanded in a lower tone.

"It'll be easier than in the United States," the big fellow replied, and after that he seemed to concentrate his whole attention on driving, for the road was rough from the rains and the boy in the back was soon splashed thickly with mud. Presently they came to the bridge which connected North Hero with Isle La Motte. Jim could see that the water had risen until it was splashing through the planking, and dozens of men were working hard to keep it from being washed away. They were bringing the biggest rocks they could haul and were distributing them in piles from one end to the other. Young Austin hoped anxiously that none of the workmen would call Burnam's attention to the extra passenger he was carrying, but they passed over quickly, and if anyone noticed the boy, nothing was done about it. They probably thought him a hiker tired of walking and unable to get a lift on his way. The car sped on to the station, but it was deserted, and Jim was mighty thankful that no agent was there to answer inquiries regarding the travelers who were supposed to have gone on to Toronto. Half a mile ahead the machine had to slow up for a sharp curve, so feeling confident that the pair were really headed for Canada, the boy dropped off and started to trudge home. A good-natured farmer gave him a lift, and at last he saw Bob anxiously scanning the road.

"Gosh all hemlock, I was going into the air to look for you. Say, come on, quick." He led the way to the water's edge, and far across the thrashing lake Jim saw a tiny boat, with an outboard motor on the stern, chugging valiantly against the waves and making for Fisher's Island.

"Who is it?" Jim demanded.

"Corso and the boy. I saw them a few minutes after they left the shore. They have a load of stuff aboard as if they intend to hide over there," Bob explained.

"Gee, I wonder if it's safe!" Jim said anxiously.

"I asked Uncle Norman and he said the greater part of the land is under water now, but there are high spots that may serve them. Let's keep an eye on the place, Jim. I think that pair is all right, and gosh, I'd hate like fury to have them carried away in this. Just look at it." Jim didn't need to look any more than he had for as far as he could see, the wreckage, large and small, was being tossed and dashed to splinters.

"So should I. We'll keep watch, then if it looks bad we'll go after them in Her Highness. I say, did you happen to notice the number of that limousine? I, like a dub, forgot to look at it."

"I wrote it down," Bob answered proudly, and he produced the figures.

"Good work. I'm going to call up Ruhel and tell him to be on the look-out for that pair. They're no good and the Mounties will keep them under observation." He hurried into the house, called long distance, and in five minutes was telling the story to the chief, who listened with interest.

"Thanks no end, Old Man. I take it you'd like us to let them roam around here for a while and give your friends a chance."

"That's the idea."

"We'll keep them hunting. It will do them good. Oh, by the way, I say, what time did you lads breeze in to your house this morning—"

"Don't ask personal questions," Jim retorted.

"I don't have to, I know. Mason came in this afternoon and told the story. You knights had some night. I hope they pin something on you—"

"Probably they will. We ought to have a lemon. Well, thanks for listening."

"Same to you." The connection was cut off, and Jim joined his step-brother on the veranda.

"Listen, Buddy, that watch dog Uncle Norman bought, died this morning, and now the other one is sick. What do you know about that?"

"Rotten. Wonder if there was anything the matter with them when they arrived, or if some one over there didn't want watch dogs?"

"Hezzy?"

"That's the lad I'm going to keep an eye on. Gosh." He jumped to his feet and started to walk toward the garden. "For a quiet little place, we surely have found no end of excitement since we landed."

"It hasn't been exactly dull," Bob admitted. They went on in silence and at last they reached the edge of the alfalfa meadow. The stones the strange boy had been working with a few days before were neatly arranged in a low wall, and the land above was terraced as if by someone skilled in the art. The whole section which the Fenton's had called the bog had been plowed, smoothed on a slight incline toward the lake, which left the garden side lower than that land, and this also was built up with a cleverly set curb of stones. There were three small outlets which acted as drains, and in spite of the heavy rains the land was comparatively dry.

"Well, anyway, your uncle has got this work to be thankful for. It sure looks like a grand piece of land. Perhaps he can plant it with something that he can harvest this season. Must be odd to be in a place where the summers are as short as they are here. I'd like to see it in the fall. It must be quite a sight."

"I'd like to see it in the winter. Mom says the lake freezes over, and the people who live near cut ice, and they can cross to New York, or any place they want to go. They drive, have races and skate," Bob volunteered.

"We can't stay to see all that," Jim said regretfully. "The parents wouldn't stand for it."

"No, I know it."

"Supper," Mr. Fenton called, and the boys made their way back to the house. They were very thoughtful as they took their places, and the food was eaten in silence.

"Any more turkey's stolen, Uncle Norman?"

"Some were taken last night," the man answered. Just then the telephone rang and Aunt Belle answered.

"The Norman's are going to stay here all night," she said quietly. "Their house is flooded above the kitchen."

That evening Stumble Inn was filled to the brim with neighbors. Belated supper was served to refugees who straggled in, and the two boys turned to and helped. They carried down cots, made beds, washed dishes, turned horses into the pasture, and drove cattle into the meadow. It was late at night when they were repairing a place in the fence to be sure that the nervous stock did not break through and get away. When the job was finished, they made their way back to the house, and all along the road they could see tents pitched, or families gathered about their cars or wagons prepared to sleep out of doors. The protection they had was frail and if another storm should come up suddenly half their worldly goods would be swept into Champlain.

In spite of their dilemma the Vermonters were facing their troubles quietly and without a whimper. Although there were as many as fifty people within earshot, hardly a sound could be heard. Then a child, whose sleeping quarters was under the big maple, cried in fright. The mother tried to hush it, but the little fellow's terror did not diminish. Without an instant's hesitation, Bob leaned over the wagon.

"Don't be afraid, little fellow. You come on in and sleep—"

"There isn't any room in your aunt's house, Bob," the woman answered. "She would have taken us if she could."

"Come along anyway," Bob insisted. He picked the boy up in his arms, while Jim offered to help the woman.

"I'll be all right here," she answered, "if you can find a place for the children." A little girl raised her head.

"Come on, Old Man," Bob urged. The boy came to him willingly, and the girl reached her arms out to Jim. Together the two went to the house. The living-room door was wide open, and there were beds spread out on the chairs as well as the floor.

"I put some more beds in your room, boys," Aunt Belle said softly.

"Anyone in our cots?" Bob asked.

"No," she answered.

"We'll put the babies on them, Aunt Belle. You don't mind, do you?"

"Of course not, Bob, but where will you sleep?"

"Oh, in one of the hammocks—"

"You can't, my dear, they are all full."

"We'll find a place. Aunt Belle, maybe you'd better come along. We don't know much about little fellows." They started to climb the stairs and his aunt followed. It did not take long for the little codgers to be tucked in comfortably, and in a moment they were both asleep. It seemed to the boys as if the very air was charged with impending danger as they went down stairs again. Some of the Vermont men and women were sitting around on newspapers on the lawn. They spoke softly, partly because of their friends trying to rest, and partly because they were making a brave effort to face the disaster courageously.

"Heard that no more trains can get through," one man remarked.

"Ed Allen's prize sheep ran into the lake and were carried away," said another.

"Something frightened them."

"The lower end of Canada is in a bad way. The border men asked for all the milk they could get, even if it's sour."

"Expect we better do some sort of organizing and see what we have," another proposed. "Let's talk it over with Fenton." The boys moved on and sat down against the shed.

"Say Jim, know what this makes me think of, these people I mean?"

"Makes me think of so much, I'm getting brain-storm," Jim answered, but his tone was sober.

"The history we read—these Vermonters. Those Allen boys. Did you know the two towns, North Hero and South Hero are given those names because of the brothers, and a lot of their original tract of land is still in the families' possession?"

"I heard your mother say so. They were a great gang."

"Sure were. Well, I was thinking how these people, some of them members of those old families, still stand shoulder to shoulder. Of course most folks are pretty decent when neighbors are in trouble, but here they are also quiet and sure of each other. No wonder they are considered a fine lot. A couple of hundred years ago just a handful of them bucked against the hardships and won out. Now, Uncle Norman and Aunt Belle are facing ruin maybe, but they are right with their neighbors, ready to share everything they have as long as they have it—you see what I mean—it's a great spirit, I think."

"So do I. I say, let's see if we can find a couple of blankets and sleep out here," Jim proposed.

"Suits me," Bob agreed. They had no trouble finding bedding and soon they were ready to turn in. Before they did, they stood staring off across the black water of Lake Champlain.

"I say, isn't that a light over there on Fisher's?"

"Was just watching it. Perhaps it's Corso's fire. Gosh, that means they're all right and I'm glad of that." They watched the tiny streak of red that burned cheerily in the darkness, but finally they stretched out and were soon asleep.

XI
THE CRY FOR HELP

Neither of the boys slept soundly that night. Their dreams were troubled by a conglomeration of their experiences since their arrival at North Hero, the weird boom of the waves as Champlain rose steadily, and a confusion of people going by in search of places of safety. Several times men stopped to inquire for lodgings or routes, and it seemed as if a dozen dogs howled gloomily. But above it all, toward morning, there was one sound that came to their subconscious minds and they stirred fitfully as if trying to shake off a nightmare. Then suddenly they awoke and sat up. It was still dark, that pitch darkness that is so thick just before the first streaks of dawn brush the sky.

"I say, Buddy, did you hear anyone call?" Jim whispered.

"I was just going to ask you the same question," Bob answered. "I thought I heard a cry for help." They sat listening tensely, straining their ears to distinguish the call that had broken into their sleep, but could make out nothing more than the sighing of the wind through the bowing trees and the noises they had been hearing before. Jim started to slip into his shoes and Bob followed his example.

"Let's get some clothes on, I can't sleep any more, can you?"

"No. Gosh, Jim, this is spooky." They slipped their trousers and sweaters on over their pajamas, without stopping to don shirts. In two minutes they were dressed and made their way carefully to the rim of the water. "We'd better have a flashlight or we'll be stepping into it."

"I've got the little one in my pocket." Jim took it out and pressed the button. Its faint tray cast a round glow, not very bright, but sufficient to show them where to step. Austin led the way while Bob followed close at his heels and finally they stopped on the edge of a cliff and stood listening tensely. For what seemed like an hour, although it was less than a minute, the world was oddly hushed, as if it too were listening, then, clear and unmistakable from north of them, somewhere on the lake, came a terrified cry and a shout for help.

"Let's get Her Highness. Somebody's out there," Bob whispered, and as fast as they could they ran to the carriage shed, where the plane was bumping the top of her wings on the high roof of the ceiling. In order to get inside the boys climbed through the window on the opposite end, and even then had to wade ankle deep in water. They lost no time in getting ready, just enough to be sure that all was well and there was plenty of gas in the tanks.

"All O. K.," Jim announced taking the pilot's seat.

"Right with you. I say, Old Man, we never can hear anything with the engine going, and we can't see much through this pitch."

"I know it, and we don't dare stay on the water or we are likely to get a tree in the works, but we've got to take a chance. That voice sounded as if it's a little north, didn't you think so?"

"Yes, and sort of far away—muffled." They floated out into the cove, all lights on, and Jim gasped as he saw that the wind had changed during the night and the water on that side was dangerously full of wreckage. He set his lips grimly, opened the throttle, raced out over great rollers that teetered them even more than the day they returned from Burlington in the storm. Her Highness lost no time in lifting herself above the danger and soared up two hundred feet as her nose was brought about and her course was set north by north west.

Anxiously Bob leaned over as far as his safety-strap would permit and scanned the blackness beneath them hoping to catch sight of something which would account for what they were seeking. Jim sent the plane in wide circles in order to give Bob a chance to see as far as possible, and although their lights helped some, they seemed to make the rest of the night even darker. For ten minutes they rode in a fruitless search, each time coming around a little further north.

"Jim, things I can make out are being carried fast toward the south. Perhaps we're too far up," Bob said through the tube, and Jim nodded. He changed the procedure, while the younger boy watched. Five minutes more they circled, then Jim decided to climb. He tipped Her Highness' nose at a sharp angle and zoomed two thousand feet just as fast as she could scramble through the air, then he shut off the motor and let her glide. The lake beneath them seemed a regular bedlam of sound, and as they drifted forward at as gradual a descent as possible, they finally picked up a frantic call.

"It's over there," Jim exclaimed and his buddy agreed. The plane was so low now that they dared glide no longer, so Jim set the engine going full blast as they made for the place.

"There's a light." Bob clutched his arm and pointed. Whoever had cried out evidently had some dry matches or a cigarette lighter and was trying to help them locate him. In a moment they were riding in close circles, and then they made out what looked like the roof of a portable summer house. They couldn't tell what was on top of it, but by that time the morning light began to break slowly.

"What the heck can we do?"

"Tie the lariats together," Jim directed. That was but the work of a moment, then Bob put a weight on one end of it and threw it over.

"If he can grab it, we can give him a tow." Jim nodded, so Bob leaned over again. "Come a little lower." Her Highness obeyed, and with the help of the speaking tube, they at last managed to get the plane in proper position, and almost instantly there was a tug as the rope was caught. It was evident that since they had come to him the stranded man had been using his head, for he managed to keep from being dragged off the roof, and even made the end of the lariat fast to a rod that stuck out near the metal chimney.

"She's coming," Bob shouted—"Go easy or she'll be banged to bits."

Sturdily Her Highness taxied forward just as low as she could. Bob kept his eyes on the house they were towing, and several times he caught his breath sharply as a particularly heavy plank, a broken tree, or a drowned animal came thumping into it. As it got lighter, the boy was amazed to see that the roof held more than just the man, who had flung himself on his face, his body sprawled out flat as he kept a woman and a tiny baby from being jarred off.

"Oh, great guns," Bob whistled.

"Throw off the line," Jim directed. They were in the cove now, and already Mr. Fenton and several men were on the shore, while two strong young fellows were in the row boats, prepared to shove out and help. The waves battered them all angrily, but Her Highness had to soar up out of the way, and after a few minutes in the air where she waggled her wings gaily over her victory, she was brought down again, and the Flying Buddies hurried to learn about the man and his family.

"Are they all right, Aunt Belle?" Bob called as they went into the kitchen.

"Yes. Here, you hold the little fellow a minute, while I stir this." She promptly dumped the baby into her nephew's arms, and Jim grinned at his brother's discomfort.

"Will it break, Mrs. Fenton?"

"Break—" She looked at Bob and laughed, "No, certainly not, if it can come alive through such a night. They were driven to the roof hours ago because the floors of those cottages are fastened to the ground and can't get away—"

"I don't know how I can ever thank you fellows—" said the rescued man as he came into the kitchen.

"Aw, please don't try. We thought we heard you call, so we went to see what it was all about," Jim said quickly, but he had to take the hand that was extended to him.

"If I had been alone I wouldn't have howled, but with my wife and baby I had to do anything I could. We were asleep, and it seemed as if an earth-quake gave us a broadside and we were full of water. We just managed to get some blankets to keep the baby warm, and climb through the window. We were on the veranda roof first, but that wasn't very secure, so we got on the main part. It was good we moved, for the other sections were battered off—"

"My land sakes alive—how awful. Here now, you take this in to your wife and tell her to drink every bit of it like a good girl, and just as soon as I get some more dry things on the baby, she can have him back. He is a cunning little fellow—" Bob was no end relieved that his services as a nurse were no longer required.

"Buster," he chuckled as he handed the baby to his aunt.

"My land sakes alive. How did you boys happen to get that man and his folks? I never saw the like—never. I thought you were asleep by the barn, and then, all of a sudden, some one said you were out down the lake and you were coming in slow like. Fent got the glasses and saw those folks—my land sakes alive, I never saw the like of it. How did you happen to be out there?"

"We couldn't sleep, and we thought we heard someone call, so we went out. Reckon we better get dressed, we haven't got much on," he added, because several people were trooping into the kitchen and he didn't want to be the center of an admiration meeting.

"Come down as soon as you're ready and have breakfast. You must be most starved both of you." There is nothing like an early morning rescue party to sharpen the appetite, so the boys did not take long to get ready. Jim went down first and just as he came into the living room, the telephone, which was a party line, gave a long persistent ring.

"That's forever ringing," Mrs. Fenton called to him. "Will you answer it? I can't put down the baby for a minute."

"Glad to." Jim took down the receiver and heard the operator.

"Please do not try to use your telephone until further notice, unless the call is very important. The lines are congested. The Selectmen have given orders that no one is to try to cross the bridges—either at the north or south end of North Hero Island. Please tell people on the road they cannot go any further." The girl repeated the same thing three times to be sure that everybody got it, then there came a click as she closed the connection. Austin gave the message to Mrs. Fenton, who sighed heavily.

"My land sakes alive—there, there, you are almost ready, little fellow. This is a nice baby! Now you can go to your mother." She hustled the infant to his parents and then hustled back to serve her hungry household. During the meal two serious-faced men came to the house.

"We heard that your nephews dragged in a family that might have been drowned, Fent," one of them started.

"Yes they did," Mr. Fenton admitted and introduced the boys to the men, who shook hands gravely.

"I've heard that there are some families stranded on the islands, and it may be that some of the summer colonies have suffered just as that family you brought in. We were wondering if you will help us get any others, if there are any. We have several good strong power boats, but we would waste a great deal of time trying to locate people and might not find them all."

"If you will fly around and watch for signal fires or flags, then we could send the boats directly and take them off," the other added.

"Of course we'll be mighty glad to help," Bob declared promptly.

"Thank you. Another thing, there may be some who haven't had much to eat for a couple of days, not being able to use their boats. Could you drop food to them?"

"Sure thing," Jim replied. "We'll take some weights along because we don't usually carry anything like that. We just happened to have one this morning or we might not have been able to give that fellow a tow."

"Thank you. We'll arrange to have boats and rafts at four points of the island. If you find anyone, give the word to the nearest party. I'll show you about where they are." He took a map from his pocket and pointed to four places that would be used for stations. "You can come down on the water to speak to the men we'll have there?"

"Yes, we'll manage."

"That will be good. We appreciate your help." Then he turned to Mrs. Fenton. "My wife and some of the neighbors in the village are packing boxes of food, sandwiches, coffee and milk. We'll send a truck—it ought to be here in a quarter of an hour—and the boys can take it with them and use their own judgment about dropping it."

"I can fix them some—"

"Judging by the number of people you have taken in I think that you are doing your share, Mrs. Fenton. We won't ask you to do any more," the man replied. "Now, I'll telephone to the boatmen—"

"They just told us not to use the phone," Jim explained.

"They will give me a connection," the man smiled. In a minute he was giving information, directions and instructions, and finally the rescue work was well organized. By the time the boys were ready to take off, the truck appeared with boxes of food, and the chauffeur helped them store it in the plane.

"We're lucky to have you fellows here," the man said, when finally the task was accomplished.

"We're in luck to be here," Bob grinned. "My mother always said that I'd like this place, and I do."

"Come along." Jim waved to the men, opened the throttle and Her Highness tore across the cove, rose and started on her errand of mercy. She seemed to appreciate the importance of the work before her, and never did an airplane behave more beautifully. They went circling north on the lake and were about to turn when Bob shouted through the tube.

"There's a raft load, look at it!" Jim glanced in the direction his step-brother pointed and saw the crude raft being whirled like a top and it was a marvel that the thing held together. The boys saw two boys, young fellows, some household effects, and a little girl. Austin glanced at the map, picked out the nearest station, and they raced to it, coming down where the water happened to be fairly smooth.

"There's a raft out there," Bob shouted. Instantly the engine of the power boat gave a bellow almost as furious as the plane's, and off the party scooted, cutting through the waves and sending a rolling sheet of foam on either side of them. Her Highness raced back to be sure the rescuers did not miss their goal, and in a few minutes the first job was being done well.

"Not a bad stunt," Bob grinned and then the Flying Buddies started to work again. They discovered families huddled on tiny bits of land that had been cut off by the water, others on great rocks and a number on floating buildings that threatened to fall to pieces any minute. Each time they led the way for the power-boats and had the satisfaction of knowing that all were saved. About noon the four power-boats were out, besides several smaller motor-boats and the boys spied two more families stranded helplessly, so they decided to drop food.

"I'll tell them the men will come for them," Bob announced. He proceeded to write the message in the box and dropped it over. In that particular group they counted ten people, so they dropped more boxes. Then on they circled. The men of the party waved their thanks and an hour later, Her Highness returned, escorting the boats. The work went on for hours until finally one of the men at a station shouted,

"Mrs. Fenton says that you fellows must come and eat."

"We'll stay a while longer—"

"No, you mustn't. You show us this bunch, then go home and tank up. It's the Selectmen's orders and you have to obey."

"All right," Jim agreed, then he looked at the dial. It was half past one and he could hardly believe his eyes. So the orders were obeyed, and Her Highness too had to be tanked up for her gas supply was dangerously low. In the afternoon the boys went up again, and although they circled miles they discovered only two more people who needed rescuing, then Bob, who was piloting, had an idea.

"I say, Buddy, I'm going to hop down on Fisher's Island and find Corso."

"We saw them earlier and they were all right," answered Jim.

"I know, but they might not be by morning. Let's just make sure."

"Suits me," Jim acquiesced. Her Highness was brought about and was soon circling over Fisher's Island, which was more than half submerged, but it did not look as if anyone on it would be in any immediate danger. Soon Bob picked out a landing spot on an open space where the ground was high and fairly smooth. Presently the plane was on the ground, and the boys began to look about. It did not take them long to locate the foreign man, who came to meet them.

"Burnam left?" he questioned anxiously.

"He surely did. Went on to Canada, and he can't get back because both bridges are closed until the flood goes down," Jim explained.

"It is good that he is gone, but we cannot get away," Corso said, and he scowled thoughtfully. "It may not be many days before he discovers that you tricked him, then he will come back. He is very determined."

"I guess it must be pretty bad with you if you feel that way," Bob put in quickly. He couldn't help wondering why the man was afraid.

"It is much bad, Sirs."

"Tell you what, we'll take you across to New York. Will that help?" Jim offered cordially.

"It would be much help. Come." He led the way through a strip of woods and around a boulder, where the man stopped, gave a low whistle, waited for a response, then they went on and in a minute they came to a well sheltered spot where the trees grew high and thick and the cliff formed a semi-circle protection with an overhanging top.

"Whew," whistled Bob in astonishment. Back from the opening stood the mysterious boy, straight as a die, but instead of overalls and brown shirt, he wore a long white garment of some very fine material, and over that was a richly embroidered coat, brilliant with peacock-feather trimming. On his head was a deep fringe arrangement and at his feet a strong box. The lid was open and its contents made the brothers think of some Arabian Night treasure.

"You signaled, my uncle!" He spoke in perfect English, and the man answered, briefly in their own tongue, whatever that was. "It is well," the boy nodded. Then he turned toward Jim and about his lips was a faint smile. "It was considered best that I do not permit it to be known that I understand your language."

"Holy Hoofs, and we were being little helpfuls trying to teach you," Jim exploded.

"You have been most generous to us, also the Fentons."

"Well, we're glad to have been," Bob replied a bit weakly.

"My uncle knows men and I too recognize those who are trustworthy, even though I am only twelve years old—"

"Only twelve. Why, you are as tall as I am."

"Today I am twelve. Because of your great kindness I shall impart to you a little about the reason I am here, if you are interested—"

"I say, we've been busting to know ever since we first saw you, but you needn't tell us a thing unless you want to," Jim assured him.

"You need bust no longer." Across the boy's face a smile flashed. "Let us be seated. We shall be free from interruption." He spoke as if he were some great personage giving an audience, but there was something about his whole bearing that made the step-brothers have perfect faith in him. They seated themselves on the ground close to him, while his uncle stood on guard.

"Maybe you better close this," Bob suggested. "We didn't see anyone else on the island, but you never can tell. Is that what Burnam's after?"

"Burnam is after much more than this," replied the boy, and he dropped the lid, shutting the contents from sight. "I was born in a far land. Its name I shall keep. Five hundred years ago my people were great rulers of a happy nation. It was ruthlessly invaded, conquered, and great works wantonly destroyed. A few of my fathers escaped destruction, they tried to get back their land but their efforts were fruitless. Later, they united secretly and hid their vast treasure which the conqueror could never find. They kept together generation after generation, although few outsiders are aware that any of the pure blood are alive." The boy paused, but his audience made no comment.

"In my conquered land there is a beautiful statue to one of my blood who fought successfully and helped free the nation from the devastator's yoke." A gleam of pride shone in the boy's eyes.

"Did they get it back?" Bob whispered.

"No, but they got rid of the—the yoke. In the generations the number of men of my race has grown. It is now like a vast army, secretly governed by wise men. Many are scattered in different countries, learning the best of the white men's way of living, keeping the best of their own knowledge of life. There are still parts of my country that are unsettled, and one day we shall unite there. We shall be versed in the greatest sciences, and never again can we be conquered or put to rout by ignorance or brute force—we shall be the conquerors, and we shall rid ourselves of the waste races as your uncle rids the garden of rank worthless weeds that would choke and smother the good about them." There was no malice in the boy's tone, no bravado in his manner, he spoke impersonally and without bitterness. His eyes shone with a fine intelligence, he made his statements quietly, and once his eyes wandered to the horizon as if they beheld that future.

"Accurate records are being kept by every generation and brought together. I have been taught the ancient arts of my fathers, I have worked with the soil as my fathers did, and now that I am twelve years old, I am ready to study the sciences, the languages, higher mathematics—the classics." He broke off a moment, then went on. "I may not live to see the establishment of my race, it may not come for hundreds of years, but it will come when we are fully prepared to take the reins and hold them firmly." His eyes rested first on Bob, then Jim. "Whether it is years hence, or centuries, because of what you have done for one of our princes, the men of your tribe, James Austin, and of yours, Bob Caldwell, will be spared, even though they be inferior, they will be given a chance. I have spoken, and my uncle has written it into the records."

"Gosh," Bob gasped. "If they aren't any good, don't bother with them." His face flushed suddenly, he didn't know why, but he felt that weeds of all kinds should be destroyed.

"Now, before you take us to New York, I will give you each a token. Give it to your son, and your son's son, and on, for one day it will find its way back to my land." He opened the box, drew out two large green stones. They were oblong in shape, some marks had been worked into them, and into a groove in one side was a tiny many-colored tube of exquisite enameling. The boy pressed an invisible spring and the tube opened revealing a slip of parchment covered closely with fine writing.

"I say—" Jim started to protest, but the boy paid no attention to him.

"Keep these always, they are fine emeralds. Here are smaller pieces." He picked up two rings. "Wear these and wherever you are seen by any of my people you will be helped and protected." He handed the jewels to his amazed companions, then went on, "Mr. Fenton has been losing his turkeys. Watch the man who is taking care of them, watch him closely."

"Thundering rattlers, is he the thief?"

"He is a naturally dishonest man. Watch him closely and you will learn what happened to the turkeys."

"Thanks a lot, old man—gee, Uncle Norman will be no end obliged to you, and gosh, he is already, for that bog you drained is still dry—"

"It will remain dry—" the boy assured him.

"Maybe we'd better be starting," Jim suggested, "that is, if you are in a hurry to get to New York."

"We shall be glad to hurry."

"I say," Jim put in, "You know, maybe I'm a nut, but if you people, I mean you and your uncle, would kind of act like ordinary people, not wear anything that looks a bit different, or act as if you are trying to keep out of sight, you wouldn't attract attention—nobody would pay any attention to you at all, except maybe in a little place like North Hero, where everybody knows everybody else," he finished hurriedly. The boy sat thoughtfully for a moment, then he smiled and held out his hand.

"Thank you, it is excellent advice."

"When you are by yourselves you can act naturally, I mean as you do anyway, but you look as if you are different, you seem to know more—"

"Thank you, we will do that, and I hope we meet again, Jim Austin and Bob Caldwell."

"If you come to Texas, look us up. This is where we live." He gave the boy a card, with the address scrawled on the back.

"We will get ready," Corso interrupted.

"Well, I say, where does this Burnam come in?" Jim asked.

"He was employed to do some task for one of our people and he suspected that somewhere great wealth must be stored. He saw me once in my father's house. When his work was done, he was paid and dismissed, and taken away, so that he could not find the place again, but he came upon my uncle and myself on your western coast. He believes that I know the secret and tried twice to kidnap me, but he has failed each time, and he will fail again, for it is written in the forecasts that I shall live to a great age and that my enemies shall perish. One day you found a box, it held knotted strings. Long before writing, or signs, tribes made their records by that method, I know the language of the knots in the colored strings."

"Why, I've read of that, learned it in school, old language," Bob exclaimed with enthusiasm.

XII
DETECTIVES

"I say, what a pair of nuts we are. We don't know that boy's name." Jim, who was in the passenger seat beside his step-brother, made the announcement with disgust. Bob made a grimace.

"We do take first prize. Do you think that pair are batty?"

"Not as batty as some of the rest of us," Jim declared emphatically.

"That's what I think. I say, let's not do any talking about them. You know, sometimes a little thing starts things and evidently this Burnam bird isn't letting any grass grow under his feet."

"That's a first-rate idea." They had just left Corso and his nephew in one of the small towns in the northern part of New York state, and the couple had taken a train south. Now the boys were about ready to return to North Hero.

"I'm telling the cock-eyed world that we are landing on the turkey farm and somebody's going to talk turkey. It won't be us," Bob declared.

"Atta boy. You know, Buddy, we agreed with what that boy said just because we've been suspicious of Hezzy all along, but we couldn't convince your uncle nor any of the Selectmen on anything as thin as that. We've got to get something on the fellow; something no one will be able to think isn't really proof."

"That's right," Bob acknowledged. "It's getting kind of late. Suppose we drop down there. If Hezzy's around we can get the lay of things, and maybe find evidence enough so Uncle Norman can act on it. We'll have to be mighty careful, or Burley will be suspicious."

"We might say we need a little gas, that our tanks are empty," Jim suggested. "And ask about the dog, if he's getting over that sickness."

"Yes, that's the idea. I've been wondering—if Hezzy is getting away with the turkeys, he wouldn't want a good watch dog around. I've got a kind of hunch we'd better be ready to act with a snap."

"Suits me. Let her go." Bob opened the throttle and presently they were in the air, each thinking soberly of what might be before them. As Jim recalled the weird experiences of the afternoon and the interview with the foreign boy, it all seemed mighty unreal, but he had to admit that the emerald ring on his middle finger was not a dream, and the jewel in his shirt pocket pressed against his chest was substantial enough. The air was heavy with clouds that hung low, and the boy knew that another storm was brewing. He hoped it wouldn't be a bad one, for the Vermonters had already suffered terrific loss because of the late rains and the flooding lake which was sweeping everything before it. Looking down he could see the thrashing waves, and the whimsical idea came to him that the lake was determined to go somewhere.

"A river has more fun," he grinned to himself. Bob's mind was fully occupied with his job of piloting, but it did not take long to cross Champlain. It was dark enough now so that homes were being lighted up. The bright window squares began to look like jewels suspended on a rapidly darkening background. In a little while night would be upon them. As they approached Isle La Motte they were riding five thousand feet up, and suddenly Jim noticed two other planes flash through the clouds from the north. He wondered if it was their friend the mail pilot, but the hour was not right, and besides there would not be two. He touched Bob on the arm, and pointed.

"There's a couple of planes." Bob picked them out a moment later, then both boys sat tense and astonished as they noticed that the flying machines were circling above the eastern side of the turkey farm. Through breaks in the mist the boys saw that the machines were both large ones, big enough to carry considerable freight or several passengers. Why they should be maneuvering through the clouds above Isle La Motte was puzzling, so Bob, as he watched them, guided Her Highness in a wide circle a thousand feet higher. He was confident their presence would not be observed or heard as long as the other engines were racing. Keeping the planes within their range of vision was difficult, and several times they lost sight of them, but succeeded in picking them up again. Jim had his eyes fast to the glasses, and suddenly he made out a man standing upright on one of the wings. A second man jumped out of the cock-pit and joined the first, then a third and a fourth got on to the other side of the fuselage. It took an instant for the boy to guess what they were going to do, then he shouted.

"They are going to jump!"

"Over the lake."

"The farm. I'm going after them." As soon as the words were out of his mouth he was busy with the safety straps, and as he unbuckled himself he noticed their lariats coiled about the hooks. Instinctively, but with no idea for what he might use them, the young ranch boy reached for the long plaited leather ropes. It was natural to have them in his hands, and he hopped out of the cock-pit.

"I'll land over there and join you as fast as I can," Bob bellowed, and although Jim could understand only one or two of the words, he guessed the rest and nodded. He glanced down again and by that time counted five figures dropping through the clouds, but instead of white silk parachutes blossoming out above them, the huge umbrellas were some dark color which was soon lost in the haze. Without waiting any longer, Jim hopped over, while Bob maneuvered to keep out of his way, then the pilot turned about and started for the nearest shore of the lake.

While dropping through the air toward the Fenton turkey farm, Jim's brain was working like a trip hammer. His parachute was white and therefore conspicuous. He did not want to land before the other jumpers nor did he want to be too near them. As soon as he was clear of Her Highness, he pulled the cord, and calling to his mind a detailed picture of the property, he guided himself far enough to the north so that he would be over the forest. He hoped that the others would be too occupied in their own arrival to do much looking around. The parachute floated him gently, and by spilling air carefully, he managed to keep from, being carried from the course he wanted to follow.

Sometimes the mist was so thick that he couldn't see a thing in any direction, and then he would be drifting through breaks light enough so that he could keep his bearings. His drop was a thousand feet more than the men he was interested in, and each one of them, he noticed, let himself go more than half of the distance before pulling the cords which opened the "chutes."

"Wow, there are more," the boy exclaimed and he counted ten tumblers. "What in heck are they up to?" He couldn't answer the question and he didn't try, but concentrated all his attention in observing as much as possible. The first man landed on the smooth space which was familiar to Jim, and he saw someone coming to meet the new arrival. The chap looked amazingly like Hezzy, and the boy whistled. He saw the fellow free himself from his trappings, then the pair scooted out of sight. By the time Jim was nearly ready to land, he had seen the ten drop out of the fog, and each one scooted away as quickly as possible. The boy glanced beneath and saw he was coming to what looked like a grove of young maples or willows, and he smiled with satisfaction. They were not very tall and promised him a safe landing. In a moment more it was made, then he too ducked out of the straps as fast as his fingers could unbuckle them. Expertly he folded the "umbrella" and hung it where he could find it again, then made his way stealthily toward the clearing. The fog was rolling from the east but did not seem inclined to settle, and that helped him a lot. At the edge of the woods, his lariat in hand, he stood trying to pick out the spot on which the men had landed. At last he discovered it, and he made another discovery. Just a few feet below where he was standing was the edge of a long, narrow fine-wire enclosed pen, such as were made for young turkeys on the other side of the farm.

"The mystery begins to clear," he muttered softly.

Stepping carefully so he would start not the slightest commotion he made the way toward the pen, and then he saw there was a shelter over a large section. The place was built of old boards and seemed to have been made to appear as inconspicuous as possible. Listening tensely,

Jim was sure that he could hear the queer noise young turkeys make, but he didn't dare to scrutinize more closely. He was determined to find where Hezzy and the ten men were located. It occurred to him that they might be already making their way to the old farm house, which was certainly big enough to accommodate them all without crowding, but at the same time he had a hunch that an investigation of his immediate surroundings would be more to the point for the present.

Before going any further Jim listened for the planes, but not an engine roared in the skies. He thought that the two had proceeded away from the place as soon as their passengers discharged themselves and the boy wondered if these men landing on Isle La Motte had anything to do with the gang which Allen Ruhel and Bradshaw had raided. The officers had said that a few got away, but of course they could not know how many. These might be left-overs who had been compelled to keep in hiding until they arranged for a safe get-away from Canada. The more he thought, the more suppositions flashed through his brain. Suddenly he heard a muffled step, as if made by a man walking cautiously in rubber boots and the boy dodged quickly behind the biggest tree, then dropped to his stomach and made a tiny opening in the underbrush so he could look through. For a breathless minute he waited, then into his range of vision came two men, one wearing an all-over aviation suit.

"One of the ten," Jim grinned to himself, "and friend Hezzy." They were coming toward the pen, and the poultry man's face was black with scowls.

"I got them here all right," he muttered, "But how can I get them away? Where in blazes is Pedro?"

"Now, keep your shirt on, can't you? You've got the birds, nobody knows a thing about them, and we'll get them away as fast as we can. I don't know where Pedro is, I told you, but I think he's in the States here somewhere. One of the boys discovered that the Mounties, blast them, are hanging around the ravine. We can't go in it, but we do know that some of the gang went off with the Canuck. He's probably helping to keep them under cover. You look after your end here—"

"Well, I've been looking after my end, but blast it all, how can I keep the gang—ten new ones, under cover? The islands are half of them under water. Know what that means?"

"Sure, they won't be bothering you," the air-man answered promptly.

"That's where you ain't got a grain of sense. There's probably a hundred people got their homes washed from under them. Everybody will be making room for them—and there isn't a house in Isle La Motte will take care of so many. The Fenton's will offer it—if they haven't already fixed to fill it up," Hezzy growled furiously.

"Whew, that's so, but they ain't likely to bring 'em across tonight, that's sure. They can't use the bridges even to walk on, and no North Hero man will bring a boat across until the lake isn't so rough, that's a cinch. You sit tight and keep a watch so you can slip 'em out if anyone shows up. This'll be a grand place to stay tonight, and in the morning some of the planes will be back, then we can make a get-away, part of us, before daylight. What do you want to do over here?"

"See that the water pans are filled," Hezzy replied sullenly.

"All right, go to it, I'll cross to the house and catch up with the other fellows. Don't hang around too long—"

"I gotta see they're all right for the night or they'll be dying on me," Hezzy insisted. The pair separated, and Jim watched the strange man strike off through the dusk, while the poultry man made his way further along the turkey pen.

"Now," whispered Jim. He jumped to his feet as nimbly and quietly as a cat, and tip-toed after the air-man. Half a dozen plans bobbed into the boy's mind, but none seemed feasible. If he could only capture the pair while they were separated he might accomplish something, but how, was the question. He hesitated a moment as he thought of going back and fastening Hezzy in the temporary turkey house, but that didn't seem good because he was sure the man could break his way out. By that time the stranger was almost across the clearing, and then the boy made a decision. Swiftly he ran, being careful to make no noise, and as he drew closer the lariats in his hand were being looped into shape. It was only the work of a moment to coil one, then taking a quick jump forward, the boy cast the loop. It swished low along the ground straight to its goal, rose over the fellow's foot as he made a step, then jumping behind a small tree, the boy jerked it taut and the chap went down on his face with a hard thump.

"Hope he landed on a rock," Jim muttered as he hauled it expertly.

It was evident that the fellow had knocked the wind out of himself in his fall, for he did not struggle, and in a second Jim was standing over him, trussing him tightly like a chicken.

"He—grr—" Austin's handkerchief was stuffed into his mouth just in time to prevent further explosives.

"Grr, yourself," Jim grinned pleasantly. At last assured that the fellow was helpless, the boy rolled him to a tree, and fastened him to that so he could not get away. "Now, ta-ta," he said softly, and taking a last glance at the knots, he hurried back toward the pen where he hoped to capture the unsuspecting Hezzy. He wished he had another rope, but he hadn't, so he picked up a good stout stick and a couple of rocks. Thus armed, he ran at top speed, then he stopped suddenly and gasped. He saw Hezzy was not alone. There was another chap with him, and the other chap was putting up a rattling good fight, although Burley was bound to be the victor. Down the pair went and Jim recognized that pair of arms and legs. It was Bob. In a moment he would be out.

"Howling pole cats," Jim yelled. Hezzy glanced over his shoulder toward the new attacker, but the stick came down on his head with a sickening thud and he stretched out beside his would be victim.

"Little Jimmy, my brother. Let me kiss you—"

"I'll knock your block off. How did you happen to get into the scrap?"

"Was coming valiantly to save you from destruction when I stumbled on this pen." The boy got to his feet, then sat down on his enemy. "Started to do a bit of rubbering when our esteemed friend arrived. He was very rude, in fact be promised to send me to hell, I believe he called the place."

"Thoughtful of him. Well, I've got the big boss, I think, tied up back there with our ropes. Better let me have your belt so we can arrange Hezzy as safely." Belts and neckties were used to secure the man's hands and feet, and into his mouth was stuffed a gag to keep him from getting boisterous, then the step-brothers took a minute to discuss the situation.

"Tell you what," Jim proposed finally. "You go back for Her Highness, and land her down here. I'll strike a match so that you can drop close, then we'll give these boys a ride to North Hero. The Selectmen can lodge them in jail away from all danger, and somebody else can come later and collect the gang in the house."

"Guess that's the brightest plan, Buddy," Bob agreed, and he set off to get the plane. Half an hour later they dropped down in the cove, and as one of the Selectmen was at the Fenton's, he heard the charge, and arrested the pair without further ceremony.

"My land sakes alive, Bob, why, it just don't seem possible Hezzy—"

"Well, we have the goods on him, Aunt Belle, and let me tell you something. There are hundreds of turkeys in that pen over there, guess your loss won't be so bad after all. Gosh, I'm glad—"

"Well—er—gosh, Bob, I am too—now then, there goes the telephone. You answer it, I'm so excited I can't talk straight." Bob went, and after listening a moment he repeated.

"Yes, now, is this right? You have a telegram from Texas, that five thousand dollars has been deposited in the Burlington bank for Mrs. Fenton because my mother, that is, Mrs. Austin, read of the flood and thought her sister could use it. Right?" A pause, "Thanks!" The boys hung up and turned to his aunt who was leaning helplessly against the door frame. "Get that, Aunt Belle!" She gave a little choking sob, and big tears ran down her cheeks.

"Yes, Bob—I did—that's just like your mother—she wouldn't even take the—time to find out if we needed it—b-but just sent it so we could have it—"

"Of course," Jim laughed. "That's just like her, I know. She's bully."

"My land—why my land, you haven't had a bite of supper, you must be starved." Then she flew about to get it ready and Bob turned on the radio.

"Weather report. Fair and warm, tonight and tomorrow," he announced.

"Good news," Mr. Fenton remarked as he came into the room.

"We've got so much good news," his wife beamed. But before the boys got a chance to eat the meal, the Selectmen came, three of them, and asked to be taken across to Isle La Motte. They wanted to round up the men in the old house before they could get away, so Jim took them over. There wasn't even a fight, and it didn't take the officers long to learn that the ten were men who had come across the border without authority, and they were hand-cuffed, placed under guard, and held for deportation.

"We're much obliged, young man," one of the Selectmen smiled at the boy and held out his hand. "You've done a lot for all of us and we hope that you will stay with us as long as you can."

"Oh, thank you. If you don't need me any more, I'll fly back or Bob won't leave me a smell of supper."

"Fly away. I think by morning the bridges will be safe so we can use them, but if they are not, and you'll pay us a visit here, I'll be further in your debt—yours and the plane's."

It didn't take long for Jim to get home, and he found that there was still plenty to eat. When he had "tanked up" comfortably, he glanced at the green emerald ring on his finger, then at his brother.

"Say, Buddy, suppose we'll ever be lucky enough to meet that kid again?"

"I have a big hunch we will," Bob declared with satisfaction.